Costa del Murder

David W. Robinson

Discover us online:
www.crookedcatpublishing.com

Join us on facebook:
www.facebook.com/crookedcatpublishing

Tweet a photo of yourself holding
this book to **@crookedcatbooks**
and something nice will happen.

The Author

David Robinson is a Yorkshireman living on the outskirts of Manchester, northwest England, with his wife and a crazy Jack Russell Terrier named Joe (because he looks like a Joe).

David writes in several genres but his mainstay is crime and mystery. In January 2012 Crooked Cat Publishing picked up the first of his popular Sanford 3rd Age Club Mysteries, The Filey Connection. Since then a further eight STAC Mysteries have been published by Crooked Cat, more titles are planned for 2013 and 2014.

He also produces darker, edgier thrillers, such as The Handshaker and Voices; titles which are aimed exclusively at an adult audience and which question perceptions of reality.

As at June 2013, he is working on the 10th STAC Mystery, Death in Distribution.

Website and blog: http://www.dwrob.com
email: dwrob96@gmail.com

By the same author

The STAC Mystery series:

The Filey Connection
The I-Spy Murders
A Halloween Homicide
A Murder for Christmas
Murder at the Murder Mystery Weekend
My Deadly Valentine
The Chocolate Egg Murders
The Summer Wedding Murder
Costa del Murder
Christmas Crackers
Death in Distribution

Other work:

Voices

The Handshaker

The Deep Secret

Costa del Murder

A Sanford 3rd Age Club Mystery
David W Robinson

Chapter One

Flashing blue lights cut through the rainy September night. The ambulance braked for a set of lights on red, the driver checked both ways and accelerated through the junction, the siren wowing to warn other vehicles off.

In the back, Joe Murray lay strapped onto a trolley, an oxygen mask covering his nose and mouth. His breathing came in painful gasps and his left arm hurt. Unable to speak (and even if he could he would never make himself heard through the mask) he silently thanked God for the impulse that had made him give Brenda and Sheila keys to not only the Lazy Luncheonette but his upstairs apartment, too. Without them, they would not have raised the alarm until tomorrow morning when they couldn't get in. They would have called the emergency services who would have broke in and found him … dead.

The word rang round his head. It couldn't be happening. Not to him. Fifty-six was no age to hang up his teapot and hand in his whites.

But there was no mistaking the symptoms. Chest pains, spreading to his left arm, sweating, struggling to breathe and when he did catch his breath it was shallow and painful.

Heart attack!

"Brenda, help me," he had croaked into his mobile. "I'm dying."

Brenda Jump had known him long enough to know when he was not pulling her leg, or simply seeking a sympathetic ear. Giving him instructions to stay still and calm, she rang the ambulance from home, then jumped in her car and drove to the Lazy Luncheonette, arriving there a few minutes ahead of the paramedics. Somewhere along the line, she also rang Sheila Riley, their friend and fellow employee, who arrived just after the ambulance.

By then, Joe had begun to feel better, but the paramedics were taking no chances. They checked his pulse and temperature, and ran an ECG. They even pricked his thumb and checked his blood sugar despite his protests that he was not diabetic. Talking over the phone to a doctor in A & E, they eventually strapped him to the gurney and hauled him down the stairs and into the waiting ambulance, where Brenda climbed in the back with him while Sheila followed in her car.

And while he lay bound to the trolley, Brenda gave the paramedic, a young woman named Karen, his details, and Joe thought about mortality.

How could this be happening? He was fifty-six, not eighty-six. He had never been overweight in his life, and his work kept him reasonably fit. People of his age and general good health did not have heart attacks.

The truth hit him like a hammer. Men of his age did have heart attacks. Not often, but they did. Men his age died from them. Not often, but they did. Gripped by the fear of approaching eternity, the thought sent his pulse racing again.

While the ambulance hurtled along the roads, he thought about all the things he had meant to do before he died, and regrettably, discovered that they did not amount to much. He had achieved almost everything he wanted in his half century and a bit, and the things he had wanted badly would never come anyway. Like joining the police force. He had always been too short, and by the time they removed the height restriction he was too old.

And while he thought about his thin, unfulfilled ambitions, the question rapped repeatedly at his brain. Why me, why me, why me? What had he ever done that he deserved to die at such a young age?

The ambulance screamed into the A & E parking area, the back doors flew open, Karen and her driver unhitched the trolley, and hurried him down the ramp. Briefly exposed to the chilly, wet, night, he shivered, but then he was inside the hospital, zooming along under the overhead lighting, the bland walls of the corridor rushing past him on both sides.

When they stopped, he could hear them talking about him.

"Male, fifty-six. Presenting chest pains, left arm pains. Pulse irregular, breathing laboured."

"Leave him with us."

The paramedics disappeared. A young man, wearing the dark blue jumper of a hospital porter, appeared behind his head and began to wheel him along. Brenda hurried alongside him, holding his hand, trying to reassure him.

They spun the trolley round, pushed him into a cubicle. A nurse appeared, slipping her hands into protective gloves, preparing a cannula.

"Are you his wife, luv?"

"What? Oh, God, no. I'm a close friend and an employee. Getting in touch with his next of kin is, er, problematic. She lives in Tenerife."

Joe wanted to protest that Alison was no longer his next of kin, but the nurse was too busy to listen.

She leaned over him, a reassuring smile on her pretty face. "Just a little scratch, Joe."

He felt the sting of the needle bite into the back of his hand, and the cannula slide into the vein, followed by the fumbling and discomfort of the nurse strapping it to the back of his hand.

"We really should have his next of kin, you know, Mrs …?"

Again he wanted to complain, but they were taking little notice of him.

"Jump. Brenda Jump. There's nowt about Joe Murray that I can't tell you. I've known him fifty years or more. The nearest

5

he has to family in Sanford is his nephew, Lee, but we can't get him out of bed at this time of night. He has to be at work in about four hours. After Lee, there's only Alison, and like I said, she lives in the Canary Islands."

Listening in on the conversation, Joe made a rapid calculation in his head. Four hours? Lee usually arrived at six. That meant it must be two in the morning.

"I can open up myself if you let me go," he shouted, but his words were muffled by the oxygen mask.

But at least this time he had their attention and the nurse lifted the mask. "What did you say, Joe?"

"I said if you stop buggering me about, I can open up the café myself."

"You can't go anywhere until you've been seen by a doctor," the nurse told him. "Now, do you want to give me all your details?"

He scowled. "Ask Brenda. She knows it all."

The nurse replaced the mask and spoke to Brenda.

Sheila joined them soon after, but it was to be a long wait. The two women were sent out when the doctor, a young blonde woman who Joe was sure used to call into his café for soft drinks and snacks when she was a schoolgirl, examined him. They took another ECG, and more blood, and he was left waiting again.

Brenda and Sheila looked exhausted, and he felt waves of fatigue sweeping over him.

Lifting the mask away from his mouth and nose, he suggested, "Why don't you two go home? I'll get a taxi back to the café."

"We're staying here, Joe," Sheila told him, "until we know how you are and what's happening."

Just after five in the morning, the doctor returned and the mask was finally, permanently removed.

"Right, Mr Murray. We don't think you've had a heart attack, but we're not sure, so we're keeping you in."

"No way. I'm going home now."

Joe tried to swing his legs off the trolley, but Brenda stopped him.

"Use your nut, Joe, and stay where you are."

"I have to be there—"

"So you can drop dead while we're serving the draymen?" Sheila asked. "We'll be so busy delivering breakfasts we won't have time to pick you up. The café will survive without you for a day or two. Stay where you are."

"I can't leave it to Lee—"

"He manages when we're away, Joe, so he can manage now," Sheila insisted. "I'll ring Lee in half an hour and make sure he knows. He'll bring Cheryl and her friends in, and the Lazy Luncheonette will survive. Now stop behaving like a child and stay put."

Sheila's words forced another unwanted memory to the surface. Her husband, Peter, a police inspector and a personal friend of Joe's had been barely fifty years old when a double heart attack killed him.

In an effort to shut the memory out, he pointed at the doctor who had been listening to the exchange. "She just said I hadn't had a heart attack."

"No, Mr Murray, I said we don't *think* you've had a heart attack. We're not sure. We need to carry out a second blood test twelve hours after the first." The doctor checked her watch. "That's about two o'clock in the afternoon. Your breathing is poor. Your chest is clacking like a rattlesnake in a bad mood. There may be some kind of infection in there. And you're in pain with your left arm. Now for your own good we're keeping you in. Once we have the results of the second bloods, we'll know more and we can think about letting you go home, but there'll be no work for a while, so get used to it."

Joe flopped back onto the trolley. There was nothing else to do.

The wet weather, an ever-present feature after a glorious early summer, saw the Gallery Shopping Mall busier than normal when Brenda entered through its automatic doors. Early Christmas displays shone from one or two stores, catching the eye of some people, but the local press had been full of woeful tales from retailers, complaining that for the nth year in succession they were losing business to the internet. The public seating was crowded, people roamed from store to store and the cafés were busy, but in Brenda's estimation, most folk were sheltering, not spending.

After leaving Joe at Sanford General Hospital, both had decided that sleep was the order of the day, not work, and left it to Lee and his wife Cheryl, to man the Lazy Luncheonette, while they went home, agreeing to meet at Ma's Pantry, their favourite eatery, at quarter past twelve.

"Les said he would be here for about half past," Brenda reported when she joined Sheila.

"I rang the hospital half an hour ago. Just before I left home," Sheila said. "They say Joe's fine, but grumpy, and would we please give them permission to put him to sleep … permanently."

Brenda chuckled, and stirred her latte. "Never changes, does he?" Her face became more serious. "What will we do without him, Sheila? You know, if …"

"That was a question I asked myself so many times after Peter died. How will I survive without him? But I did." Sheila smiled brightly. "I don't think it's an issue with Joe, though. You'll see. He'll be back in no time, moaning at us." Again she frowned. "But if it isn't a heart attack, what is it?"

"Lifestyle." Brenda's firm tones brooked no argument. "He's stressed to hell most of the time running the Lazy Luncheonette. He dashes about like a blue-arsed fly, trying to do everything, and even when he locks up for the day, he spends hours doing the books and working out the orders for the following day. Then there are those bloody cigarettes. How many times have we asked him to stop smoking? How much grief did I give him at Windermere during the summer? He could hardly speak for coughing. He doesn't eat properly, either. The only time he gets a decent, proper meal is when he comes to your house, mine or goes to Lee's on a Sunday. The rest of the week, he lives on snacks, and microwave dinners."

Sheila chewed her lip. "And if he's not working on the café, he's fiddling with bits for the 3rd Age Club. What he needs is de-stressing." A sly smile crossed her face. "Shall we send him off to Tenerife to be with Alison?"

"What a good idea." Brenda laughed again. "First off, let's sort the club out with Les, then we can cut along to the travel agent's and see what they might have on offer." Her face took on the appearance of someone who's just had an idea. "How would you fancy a week in the sun?"

"Ooh, not half." Sheila's smile evaporated as quickly as it had appeared. "I don't know if Joe would stand for it. We usually go away in October, don't we?"

"Yes, and we get enough earache off him then. Both of us off together." A slow smile crept across Brenda's lips. "We could just book it and present him with a wossname; fait accompli."

Sheila laughed. "I'd love to see the look on his face. And it would be fun, wouldn't it? You, me and Joe. We can keep an eye on him, make sure he gets plenty of rest."

"And raid his wallet for goodies."

A look of serious intent spread across Sheila's features. "Not Tenerife, though. I was joking about that. I don't think mixing with Alison would do him any good."

"Fine with me. There are plenty of places on mainland Spain with vacancies at this time of year. Or we could look at the Balearics."

Sheila began to get excited. "I haven't been to Majorca since before Peter died."

9

"Well, why don't we go to the travel agent's after we've spoken to Les, and see what they have to offer?"

Sheila was about to answer, but caught sight of Les Tanner's imposing figure making towards them. "Here comes the captain."

Les, a former Captain in the Territorial Army Reserve, greeted them cordially, joined them, and after securing a cup of tea and a cheese sandwich, listened to the tale of Joe's overnight adventures.

"Always said it would be the death of him one day, that café. I'm surprised he hasn't handed the reins over to Lee before today. Taken a bit of a back seat. What do the medics say?"

"Nothing definite yet, Les. They don't think it's a heart attack, but they won't know for sure until later this afternoon." Sheila checked her watch. "About another hour and a half."

"Whatever it is," Brenda told him, "Joe is going to need some rest, so we need someone to take over the running of the 3rd Age Club while he's down. You were the natural choice."

"Glad you think so, Brenda." Les beamed at her. "And of course, I'd be delighted. Y'know, I've had my share of clashes with Murray, but they've never been personal. I think he's hopelessly inefficient, but I wouldn't like to see any harm come to him. First order of business will be to organise a get well message from the members to our Chairman." He bit into his sandwich, chewed and swallowed. "So what will you do with him? Sit him at a corner table in the Lazy Luncheonette and make him do crosswords all day?"

"We were just discussing that. We're going to the travel agent's when we leave here. We're thinking of taking him to Spain for a week or two." Sheila tittered. "We're not going to tell him until it's all arranged."

"Good idea. Bit of sun and sand. Just the thing after a wobbler." Les swallowed a mouthful of tea. "Look, I don't want to sound pushy or anything, but Sylvia and I have an apartment in Spain."

The women exchanged smirks. "Do you now?"

"Yes, Brenda, we do." Les appeared at his most imperiously disapproving. "Our relationship is an open secret, you know."

"Only teasing, Les. We know what you two get up to," Sheila agreed. "What were you saying about an apartment in Spain?"

"It's in a complex on the Costa del Sol. Apartmentos Ingles. There's a pool, lawns, patio area, nice bar. It's right on the seafront, too. Ideal place for a little R and R."

"Oh, that's good of you, Les," Brenda said. "How much?"

"I let Robson and Frickley have it cheap for a week last year, but for you two and Murray, it's on the house," Les replied. "With my compliments. Least I can do for the miserable old so-and-so."

Sheila appeared concerned. "Are you sure, Les? I mean we don't object to paying our way."

"Wouldn't hear of it. I pay the rent monthly from my bank. All you need is your flight, and you can get a return to Malaga for less than a hundred pounds."

The women exchanged glances again.

"You'll need to arrange a transfer from Malaga Airport, but it's only about twenty minutes away. You can get a taxi for less than fifteen euros."

Sheila said, "It sounds like a bargain."

"It's agreed, then. I'll ring the apartment supervisor and let her know to expect you on Monday."

***

After speaking privately to Sheila and Brenda, Dr McKay, a tall, gangly man in his late thirties, perched on the edge of the bed, where he could face both Joe and his two companions.

"There's good news and bad news, Joe. The good news is, you haven't had a heart attack. The bad news is, you're high on the waiting list for one and it'll hit sooner rather than later if you don't watch it."

"I don't understand," Joe replied. "I take pretty good care of myself."

"That's a different tale to the one your friends here, tell me," McKay retorted. "We think, Joe, that this is muscle strain. You've probably lifted something too heavy, a little too high, and pulled a muscle in your chest wall."

"We've warned him about lifting those trays of pies onto the top rack, Doctor," Sheila said. "He's not really tall enough."

"That's why Lee is in the kitchen," Brenda said. "Young, big, strong as an ox."

"And daft as a brush," Joe pointed out.

"If he's there, you should be using him no matter how daft he is," McKay said. "You're overdoing it. You will get better, but only with rest."

"Right." Joe threw back the sheets. "Is that it? Can I go now?"

"Oh, whoa. Not so fast, my friend. I said the muscle strain will get better, but you have other problems, and they need some attention. Your breathing, for example. When were you first told to stop smoking?"

Joe answered without hesitation. "About forty years ago. Not long after I first started."

"Very funny, but that attitude will get you nowhere, Joe," McKay told him. "Now come on. How long has your breathing bothered you?"

"I don't know, do I? Three, four years. It's got worse this last few months."

"We had a weekend in the Lake District during the summer, Doctor," Sheila said, "and he was warned then about his breathing. He's already diagnosed with COPD."

"It doesn't bother me that much," Joe complained.

"It's killing you," McKay announced. "There's something else going on in there, too. An infection probably, so I'm prescribing an antibiotic. Amoxicillin, five hundred milligrams.

One three times a day, and make sure you complete the seven-day course. Next on the agenda, stress. I've been talking to your two lady friends here, Joe, and they've told me more than you did. You're under a lot of stress almost all the time."

"I'm a businessman. It goes with the territory."

"So it does, but it shouldn't be killing you and it is. You need some downtime. Let your accountant do the tax returns. Let the bank worry about your money. Let your staff do the lion's share of the work in the café. And finally, I repeat, stop smoking."

"Oh come on, Doc. I mean—"

"No, Joe. No excuses. Pack the weed in because if you don't, that croaky chest of yours will stop giving you enough oxygen and the heart attack you haven't had will happen. Now I'm going to write to your GP with a few recommendations. I suspect there may be a touch of angina, so I'm going to recommend a coronary angiogram. When that's done, go back to your doctor, ask him to repeat his spirometry tests to check your breathing hasn't deteriorated. He needs to look at your blood pressure too. It's not seriously high, but it's higher than it should be. I want to see you in outpatients three months from now to see how you're getting on. All right?"

"No, Doc, it's not all right. I don't need all this faffing about. So I have a bad chest. It's these damp days and stupid bloody laws that make me go outside for a smoke. I'll take a few less cigarette breaks. I'll make these two lift the pies into the oven if that keeps you happy. Right now, all I want to do is go home."

"No, Joe. You will stop smoking and you will take it a bit easier. If you don't, the next thing these girls will have to think about will be your funeral." McKay looked to the women for support.

"Don't worry, Doctor. We'll make him do as he's told," Brenda promised.

McKay smiled. "Good. That's what I like to hear. Joe, this

has been a shot across the bows. Don't ignore it. Change before it's too late. Take a few bob out of your hoards of cash and take a good, long, boring holiday. Because if you don't, your next of kin will pick up that hoard of cash, and after they've paid for your funeral, they'll booze it up against the wall." The doctor stood up. "All right. You can go. Don't forget to pick up your prescription at the pharmacy on your way out."

McKay left, and Joe rolled off the bed. "Bloody quack. He ought to be struck off."

"He's giving you sound advice, Joe, and we're going to make sure you follow it."

"Ha. Are you? Let's wait and see, eh? I'll be back behind the counter first thing tomorrow morning."

Sheila and Brenda smiled at one another. "No you won't," Brenda said with a smile. "You'll be packing your cases."

"Would you two like to clear off for a minute while I get dressed …" He whirled on them. "What? What did you say?"

"First thing Monday morning, we drive over to Manchester," Sheila said. "We're on the seven fifteen flight for Malaga."

"What?"

"We're going to Torremolinos for a week, Joe," Brenda told him. "All three of us."

Chapter Two

"Good morning, ladies and gentlemen. This is Captain Moore speaking to you from the cockpit. We're currently cruising at thirty-three thousand feet and our route this morning has taken us southeast from Manchester to Birmingham where we made a slight turn and now we have a nice straight line over the Cherbourg peninsula, Western France, and down through Spain all the way to Malaga. The time in Spain is one hour ahead of BST, and we anticipate being on the ground on time, at about eleven o'clock local time. The weather in Malaga is sunny and a warm twenty degrees, forecast to rise to twenty-eight degrees by the middle of the afternoon. I'll keep you posted on our progress as we go along, and in the meantime, the cabin crew will be happy to attend to your needs."

With a familiar bing-bong chime, the PA system died off, and Joe removed his watch to alter the time. "Costa del bloody Sol," he grumbled. "What's wrong with Bridlington?"

"At this time of year, everything," Sheila said. "I checked, and the average temperature for September is twenty-four degrees."

Joe feigned surprise. "You checked on the average temperature for Bridlington?"

"I checked on the Costa del Sol, as you well know. The average temperature for Bridlington is an overcoat and two jumpers."

They were sat six rows from the front, Joe on the aisle, Sheila in the middle and Brenda at the window where she had already plugged in her mp3 player and opened up her Kindle e-reader.

With a glance at their friend, Sheila advised, "Just relax, Joe, we know you haven't had a heart attack, but remember what Dr McKay said. If you don't start to take it easy, you will have one."

"How am I supposed to relax cooped up in a sardine tin for three hours with nothing between my feet and the ground but thirty thousand feet of nothing?" He reached into his gilet and pulled out paperback copy of Conan Doyle's *Hound of the Baskervilles*. "I hate bloody flying."

"Nothing will go wrong, Joe," Sheila assured him.

"I didn't say it would. I just said I hate flying."

He had been saying much the same thing since the previous Wednesday when the hospital discharged him. Even as Brenda drove him home, he protested that he did not want a holiday in Torremolinos.

"It will do you good," Brenda had chided him as she drove him home. "Hell fire, Joe, didn't we have this conversation in Windermere at Wes Staines's wedding? We don't want to lose you. True, you're a miserable old sod and generally less fun than toothache, but you're all we have, and we'd like to keep it that way. A week in the sun won't bankrupt you, but it will see you come back a new man." Checking the traffic around them, she risked a warning glance at him. "Especially if you keep off those little sticks of poison."

Unable to win them over, banned from standing behind the counter in his café, he turned his grumbles on the selection of Les Tanner taking over the running of the 3rd Age Club, *pro tem*.

"Couldn't you have asked someone else?" he whined to his two companions when they sat him at table five and furnished him with a beaker of tea. "Alec Staines or George Robson?"

"Now, Joe, don't be like that," Brenda said from the back seat. "Les has let us have his apartment for the week."

"And neither Alec nor George have any experience at

running the club," Sheila reminded him.

The official handover came that evening at the 3rd Age Club's weekly disco in the top room of the Miner's Arms.

Waiting for the members to gather together, Joe spent a short time teaching Owen Frickley how to manage the disco software.

"Show's you how nutty it all is when they won't even let me play the music," Joe complained.

"Nah, mate, they've got it right," Owen told him. "Whether you have or haven't had a wobbler, you need to take it easy until they do this heart scan."

"The angiogram? What do you know about it?"

"Had one, haven't I?"

Owen's admission surprised Joe. Like his best mate, George Robson, Owen, a big and strong man, had worked all his life for Sanford Borough Council.

"Since when did you have a heart attack?"

"I haven't had a heart attack, have I? I've had the angio-wossname though. Chest pains, Joe. Thought it was me ticker, but it was just the arteries narrowed a bit. Too many ciggies. They put a pipe in while I was on the table. A stench, they call it."

"Stent," Joe corrected. He had spent some of his overnight stay reading up on the procedure. "You have angina, then?"

Owen dug into his pocket and came out with a small, pink bottle. "Nitro glycerine. Same stuff as they make dynamite out of. I squirt it under me tongue when I feel an attack coming on." He put the medication back in his pocket. "Trust me, Joe, it's nowt, this scan. They nick your leg then put a pipe in which goes all the way to your heart and they have a look around. You don't feel anything, but it left me a bruise where I wouldn't wanna show me mother."

"I read that one in a thousand has a heart attack while they're doing it," Joe said.

"Yeah, my doc told me the same thing, but look on the

bright side, Joe. You're in the perfect place if you want a heart attack."

"I don't want one," Joe said. "That's the point."

Once Owen was sorted out, and knew what he was doing, Joe turned his attention to the 100 or so members in the room. He and Les Tanner took the dais where Les made the announcement.

"As you're all aware, our chairman, Joe Murray, has experienced some serious health problems over the last day or two, and he's been ordered to take life a little easier. I'm sure you'll all want to join me in wishing him a speedy recovery."

Joe endured the generous applause with a blush before taking the microphone.

"Thanks, all of you. I, er, I dunno what to say other than the quacks have got it wrong as usual. There's nothing really wrong with me other than a pulled muscle—"

"Pull it a bit gentler next time then, Joe," George Robson interrupted from the back of the room. His ribald comment produced a ragged laugh from the audience.

"You'd know about that, George," Joe quipped and raised another laugh. "Seriously, folks, there's nothing really wrong with me, but I've been ordered to rest for a while, so I'm handing over the chair to Les, who will fill in for me over the next month or two." He smiled grimly at Les. "Don't get too comfortable. I'll be back."

"Now you sound like the Terminator," Julia Staines called out.

"Yeah, well someone once told me I have body like Arnie. It's just arranged a bit differently." When the fresh laughter settled down, he went on, "Like I say, I'm handing over to Les for the duration, but I'll be fine. Sheila and Brenda are doing their best to make sure I behave …"

Joe paused for the chorus of "oohs" which rippled round the room, accompanied by more laughter.

"And they're taking me to the Costa del Sol next for some

sun, sand and Sangria, courtesy of Les, who's loaned us his apartment for the week." After another brief pause to marshal his thoughts, he concluded. "So, thanks again for your messages of goodwill, and a special thanks to Les for helping out. Thank you."

Joe stepped from the dais and Owen got the evening's entertainment under way with Chris Montez's *Let's Dance*.

While a few hardier souls, led by Mavis Barker and Cyril Peck, took to the floor and Les made his way back to the side table where Sylvia Goodson waited for him, Joe crossed the floor to the bar.

"Glad to hear you're all right, Joe," said landlord Mick Chadwick. "Now, how about settling your slate?"

Joe scowled. "Ask me when I get back from Torremolinos, eh, Mick?"

"Yeah but if you've had a wobbler, you might not get back from Torremolinos."

"Don't talk bloody daft, man. I haven't had a heart attack, but if people keep hassling me, I'm likely to have one from all the stress of denying it. Besides, if I shuffle off, Sheila and Brenda will settle my slate. Now come on. Am I getting some drinks here tonight, or what?"

Mick shrugged. "I'm warning you, Joe, if you snuff it and your tab isn't cleared first, you'll be barred." The landlord grinned. "Half of bitter, is it?"

"No, better not. I'm on some pills and they might not mix too well. Gimme a glass of shandy, a gin and it and a Campari and soda."

While he waited for his drinks, several people came across to wish him well. He began to tire of their overt concern, and by the time George Robson came across, he was on the point of snapping.

"Hey up, Joe, a word to the wise—"

"For God's sake, shut it, George, before you open it. I am up to here with well-meant advice. I know to take it easy, I know to pack the weed in and eat better."

"I wasn't gonna give you any advice on your ticker, you miserable old git," George grumbled. "I was gonna tip you off about Les's apartment."

Handing over cash for his drinks, Joe raised his eyebrows. "You know the place?"

"Get us a pint of mild, Mick." Having ordered, George leaned on the bar facing Joe. "Me and Owen borrowed it for a week last year. Cheap do. Y'know. He only charged us two hundred for the place and that was peak season."

"He's letting us have it for free."

Joe's triumphant smile turned George's face even more sour. "The robbing git. Anyway, it's not bad. Two bedrooms. That's for when Sheila needs to sleep on her own." He smiled broadly. "We put 'em to good use, I can tell you."

"When don't you?" Joe asked. "So go on. What are you warning me about? Don't drink the water."

"Who cares about the water? You'll drink plenty of it no matter what. Every time you order a cuppa it's made with the local water. No, mate, it's this old biddy what lives in the block. Rita Shipstone or summat, she's called. Nosy old mare, she is. You're bound to meet her ... Unless she's snuffed it, and that wouldn't surprise me. She's like you. She's got a heart condition."

"I do not have a heart condition," Joe argued. "So what about this old woman?"

"Like I said, she's a nosy old cow. Anyway, I tumbled with this bint who runs a bar at the top of the street. Coyote's the place is called, and her name is Pauline. Husband's a big bugger, but he can't do the business anymore, so she gets it on with other blokes. Know what I mean?"

"George, the chances of me scoring with some barmaid are zip. Especially with Sheila and Brenda sleeping in the next room."

"I'm not on about your trapping off, you daft sod. I'm on

about this Rita. She twigged that I was giving it one and the cheeky sow asked me for a hundred euros to keep her mouth shut."

Joe chuckled. "You didn't pay her?"

"Did I hell as like. I told her right where she could go. She threatened to tell Pauline's husband, so I told her to go ahead. He might be a big lad, but I can go some, and I had Owen to back me up."

"Well, if she's gonna try and blackmail me, she'll have to do some serious digging."

"Yes well, that's it you see, Joe. According to the crew what keeps the place summat like, she's a poisonous old sow and she's got ways of getting information that make the police look like pollsters. Just mind what you say to her."

George wandered off and Joe picked up his drinks. "Just what I need. A week in Torremolinos that I never wanted, and a blackmailing old gossip living on the doorstep ..."

The biggest problem for the next few days wasn't as Joe expected, stopping smoking. He sneaked the occasional cigarette when he was alone, anyway. It was the non-stop round of making arrangements. Still banned from working, their watchful eye looking for traces of cigarettes on or about his person, he had spent Thursday and Friday in Sanford, arranging foreign money and collecting the other bits and pieces he might need for a week on the Costa del Sol: sun lotion, aftersun lotion, travel packs of things like toothpaste, soap, shower gel and aftershave, and then spent most of the weekend with Sheila, Brenda or both, mingled with episodes of frustration as he tried getting everything he needed into his small suitcase.

After their summer visit to the Lake District, where his shorts had come in for some criticism from the hotel management, Brenda had suggested he buy new, but he refused. He did, however, invest in a few short sleeved shirts and a new, thinner gilet, in blue denim.

Finally on their way, they endured an early morning drive through the drizzle of a grim September morning, and the usual stress of clearing security at Manchester Airport. Now settled in his seat, it seemed to Joe that since the hospital discharged him on Wednesday afternoon his life had become even more hectic, thanks to the unilateral actions of his two companions.

And even with the aircraft passing over northwest France, he remained uncertain that he wanted a week's holiday in the sun.

"You'll be fine once we get to the apartment and get unpacked," Sheila reassured him as the cabin crew began to make their way along the aisle with breakfast.

Letting down his seat tray, Joe opened the hot meal and stared glumly at the contents. "If I survive the breakfast, you mean?"

***

Wearing his denims, a shirt and thick cardigan, with a flat cap covering his head, Joe stepped out of Malaga Airport and a wall of raw heat almost knocked him flat.

"I told you to take the cardigan off," Brenda scolded him.

"How was I supposed to know?" he grumbled, taking off the garment and hanging it over the handle of his suitcase. "It was raining like hell in Manchester."

"It always rains in Manchester," Sheila reminded him. "And I blame us two, Brenda. We forget Joe hasn't been abroad for many years."

"Right," he said, and patted the pockets of his new gilet. "I'm gasping for a smoke."

"Persevere, Joe," Sheila advised. "We're here to help you break the habit. You'll thank us for it one day."

Joe muttered something inaudible, and then, in a normal voice, asked, "Where do we find our transfer."

Both women looked perplexed.

"Transfer?" Brenda asked.

"Yeah. You know, the bus that takes us from the airport to the digs."

"Oh, right. No. You only get those on a package deal, Joe. Les told us it was only about a quarter of an hour by taxi, so we didn't bother."

Joe shook his head at them. "And you call me disorganised. All right. Let's get a taxi."

Cooler in his shirt sleeves, he grabbed the handle of his suitcase and led them away from the terminal to the ranks of taxis parked along the kerbside.

Brenda hurried ahead of him and began to negotiate with the taxi driver. Joe watched as the man shrugged at her.

"Sheila," Brenda pleaded, "you speak to him. He can't understand my broken Spanish. I think my Yorkshire accent is throwing him."

Sheila took one pace forward before Joe hurried past her.

"Apartmentos Ingles," Joe said. *"Calle Jaen, en Torremolinos. Cuánto es?"*

"Ah Apartmentos Ingles? Veinte euros."

"Y con nos equipaje?"

"Si. Veinte euros."

Joe nodded. "Twenty euros."

His companions exchanged amazed stares.

"I didn't know you spoke Spanish, Joe?" Sheila commented as the driver loaded their cases into the boot and they climbed into the taxi.

Settling in the front alongside the driver, Joe replied, "I don't. But I learned enough to get me from A to B. I had to. If you remember, Alison came down with the New Delhi belly when we were in Lloret and I spent most of the two weeks on my own." Settling into the seat as the driver pulled away, he said, "That's the trouble with you Brits, you know. You expect the rest of the world to learn English, but you can't be bothered to learn their language."

"Hark at him," Brenda said. "Normally, he has trouble understanding Lancastrians."

"Yes, well they're different," Joe said as the taxi moved onto the local motorway. "They're more like aliens."

As Les Tanner had promised, the journey was quite short. Within minutes they were weaving their way through the outer suburbs of Torremolinos. Joe tried to map the route, but found he could not, and gave up as they entered the familiar zone of high rise hotels and streets lined with cafés and bars, many of them English or Irish, proudly displaying the Union Flag or a Shamrock.

Fifteen minutes after leaving the airport, the driver pulled into the kerb outside a small supermarket, and pointed to his meter, which read €19.25. Joe handed him a twenty, and as the driver fished for change, Joe smiled and shook his head.

A few minutes later, the taxi pulled away, leaving them on the pavement, with their luggage, outside Apartmentos Ingles.

Flanked either side by twelve-storey hotel blocks, Apartmentos Ingles had only eight floors, and would not have looked out of place on an English council estate. Each deck had a low retaining wall, beyond which could be seen the doors of the individual apartments. There was no sign of the swimming pool Les had mentioned, only a tarmac car park behind the supermarket, edged with occasional plants and small trees.

Approaching the entrance, glass doors slid open, rattling on ill-maintained runners, and once inside, the image of a decaying establishment was complete. The Formica and panelling of the reception area was faded and cracked, the soft furnishing, chairs and couches looked old and dusty, and the view through the windows was of the car park. Joe could see a blaze of sunshine coming through the far doors.

Behind the desk a middle-aged woman, whose nametag declared her to be Christobel, greeted them with a smile. "Good morning and welcome to Apartmentos Ingles," she said.

"Murray, Riley and Jump," Joe told her. "We're staying in Mr Tanner's apartment."

Christobel perched a pair of thick lenses on her nose and studied her computer. "Ah. Yes. Apartment 705."

There followed a few minutes of standard reception routine. She took and scanned their passports, and handed over two card keys. As she was about to explain the route to the lifts and the apartment, a younger man, tall, lean and muscular, his black hair slicked back with an excess of gel, made his way through reception, towards the rear.

Christobel called him and there was a brief exchange in rapid-fire Spanish before she said to Joe, "Juan will show you to your apartment."

With a grunt, the young man led them to the elevators.

"You speak English, Juan?" Joe asked as they squeezed into the lift.

"Si, señor. My English is very excellent."

"So what do you do, Juan?" Brenda asked, her eye roaming his tight biceps.

"Do, senorita?"

"It's señora, not senorita," Brenda said. "And I meant what is your job?"

"Ah, my job. I am the maintenance operative. All of the odd jobs I do around the place, as well as ordering the cleaners."

"So you're quite versatile?"

Juan gave Brenda a lusty leer. "Si, señora. You will find that Juan is Juan of the best." He grinned, flashing even white teeth.

Joe, too, smiled, with the feeling that in a contest between Brenda and Juan, the Spaniard would come off second best.

At the seventh floor, the lift doors rumbled open to reveal a stout, middle-aged man waiting. Dressed in white flannels, a pale blue, open necked shirt, and white Panama hat, he reminded Joe of a cricket umpire.

He beamed at them as they stepped out of the lift.

"Good morning, Colonel," Juan greeted.

The smile faded and he scowled. "Morning, Pinero." His ingratiating smile returned as he concentrated on the women. "Holgate. Colonel Thomas Holgate, late of the High Peak Rifles."

Joe offered his hand. "I'm Joe Murray, and these are my companions, Sheila Riley and Brenda Jump."

Holgate fiddled with a hearing aid and ignored Joe's handshake. "Pleasure to meet you, Mr Murphy.

Joe was about to correct him when the lift doors began to close. Holgate jammed his stick in the gap and, tipping his hat to the women, stepped in. "If you'll excuse me."

The doors closed and Juan led Joe and his companions along the deck.

"Is he a resident?" Joe asked.

"Si, señor. He is not a nice man."

"He seemed pleasant enough," Sheila commented.

"With you, señora, but not with me or the maids or any Spanish. He looks down on us and always he criticises. Not a nice man."

He jammed the key card into the slot of apartment 705, pushed the door open and ushered them in.

The blinds were drawn across the balcony doors at the far end, leaving the room in semi-darkness. Juan hurried past Joe and threw them open, admitting the glare of midday sunshine, and flooding the room with natural light.

He handed over the key card. "I do not know if you are interested, señor, but there is a barbecue at two o'clock by the poolside bar. We hold it three times a week and most of the residents and other guests will be there. It costs five euros."

"We were thinking of going shopping," Sheila said.

"Is siesta, señora," Juan told her. "Shops will be shut until four o'clock."

Joe dug into his wallet. "In that case, it sounds like a bargain." He pulled out a five and gave it to Juan.

"Five euros each, señor."

26

With a jaundiced stare Joe handed over another ten and dug into his pockets. "Here y'are, lad. Get yourself a beer." He handed Juan a two euro coin.

"*Gracias señor*. If you need anything, call for Juan."

Turning to leave he found himself face to face with Brenda, who smiled up at him.

"If we need anything? Anything at all?"

"Si, señora. Remember, Juan is—"

"I know. Juan of the best."

With him gone, Joe took in their surroundings and approved.

In contrast to the exterior and reception area, the apartment was comfortably furnished. Two large settees sat against the walls, and a hatch had been cut out of the wall separating living space and the small kitchen. In front of the hatch stood a teak dining table and four chairs, and on the dresser alongside them was a portable TV.

The bedroom doors were on the right hand wall. The large twin room had a window which overlooked the beach and sea, while the small single, Joe's room, had one that overlooked the deck access. The bathroom and toilet sat between the two bedrooms.

"Brenda and I had better get down to the supermarket," Sheila said. "We need bottled water, tea bags, milk and what have you."

Joe dragged his suitcase to the smaller room. "Make sure you've got your key. I'm gonna unpack and hit the balcony, and I might be asleep by the time you get back."

Ten minutes later, his denims exchanged for shorts, he stepped out onto the balcony and leaned on the rail.

At once a sense of peace came over him. The sea lay 100 metres away, across the promenade and wide, sandy beach. Immediately below was the pool with loungers and chairs set on lawns around it, and amongst the people there, he could make out the white Panama of Colonel Holgate.

The broader view comprised a magnificent coastal vista from Malaga to the northeast, sweeping down to the further reaches of the Costa del Sol, many miles to the southwest. The strong sunlight glinted on the dappled waters of the Mediterranean. People played games on the beach, or lay sleeping, taking in the ultraviolet, while on the broad, paved path of the promenade, traders, Moroccan or Tunisian by the looks of them, spread their wares out on large sheets; fake Louis Vuitton handbags, faux Ray-Ban sunglasses, Sony mp3 players and headphones, and copies of well-known watches. It was a familiar sight to Joe, who recalled it from holidays to the Canary Islands in the days before Alison went to live there permanently.

Out to sea, small and large boats could be seen moving here and there, and further out, a large bulker made her slow, steady way to Malaga. Above them, aircraft, their livery easy to pick out in the sunshine, cruised on final approach to the airport from which they had recently arrived.

As he looked out, the stresses and strains of the last few days, the supposed heart attack, the hospital, handing over the club to Les Tanner, and all the rush-rush to get ready for the holiday, drifted into the background and disappeared. It was as if they belonged to another Joe Murray from another land, another time.

He backed off and sat at the table, patted the pockets of his new gilet, and then remembered. This Joe Murray did not smoke.

Chapter Three

The seaward facing front of Apartmentos Ingles appeared exactly as Joe had expected of a Spanish holiday complex.

Centred on a rectangular swimming pool, lawns spread out across the width of the block and down to the promenade, where it was fenced off, and a locked gate gave access only to the residents.

"The gate is like the one at The Lakeside Manor in Windermere," Brenda reported as the three companions, sharing a lift with Colonel Holgate, stepped out of the elevator into the cooler area of reception. "You use your apartment key to let you in."

Walking out into early afternoon heat and bright sunshine bathing the lawns, Colonel Holgate gestured across the lawns to the seafront and the gate in question. "Stops the riff-raff getting in."

Slightly irritated that he had been listening in on their conversation, Joe suppressed his annoyance in favour of biting back. "Riff-raff? You mean the English lager louts who turn up week in week out."

"Bit out of date, Murphy," Holgate said, rubbing a finger over his right hearing aid. "Torremolinos has cleaned up its act. Most of the lager louts go to Fuengirola or Benidorm."

"Pity," Joe said. "I like to see a good gang of lager louts enjoying themselves. And by the way, it's Murray, not Murphy. Most people call me Joe."

"Hearing not what it was, Mo," Holgate said and fiddled with his hearing aid again. "You'll forgive me but I couldn't help noticing you're in Captain Tanner's apartment."

"Les and Sylvia are friends," Sheila explained.

"Fine chap, Tanner," Holgate declared. "Don't get enough of his sort down here. Too many overpaid working class oiks, these days. May I ask, are you related to Pauline Wiley? Runs Coyote's bar at the top of the street."

Sheila shook her head. "My name is Riley, not Wiley."

"Ah. Apologies, dear lady. Old age, you know." With a stiff nod, he turned sharp right across the front of the building.

He wandered off and Brenda disapproved. "Deaf as well as daft, the barmy old sod. Someone should teach him some modern manners."

"He's still living in Victorian times," Sheila guessed. "Many ex-military officers are the same. You can never get through to them."

Sets of tables and chairs, some with parasols, were spread about the lawns, loungers were dotted everywhere, many of them now lined up around the swimming pool, but Joe noticed that the pool itself was empty, save for two young boys, playing in the shallower, children's pool. He commented on the abundance of sun loungers, all made in white plastic, with a pale blue canvas coverings.

"School holidays are over," Sheila said. "If we'd been here three weeks ago, the place would have been crowded."

On the corner of the block was the bar, described by its overhead sign as the *Poolside Bar*. Looking over the twenty metres of grass and strategically planted plants and trees between the bar and the pool, Joe wondered aloud. "How can it be the poolside bar? It's nowhere near the pool."

"Poetic licence, Joe," Brenda said.

"Yeah? Well their licence should be revoked."

On the paved area immediately in front of the bar stood the barbecue, where Juan, now attired in a white apron and chef's hat, worked at his barbecue, cooking burgers, steaks, pieces of chicken and fish. Slightly ahead of him, on the lawns, was a double table where Holgate had joined the group already seated. When Joe and the women made for the bar, Holgate rose to greet them.

"Would you care to join us, Murray? We're the core, British residents here." He gestured at the table. "Any friend of the Captain's is more than welcome."

Joe checked with his companions who nodded. "Sure. The minute we have something to eat."

"Not ready yet, señor," Juan told him. "Another ten minutes."

"Sheila, Brenda, why don't you join the Colonel and his pals while I get us some drink."

"Fair enough," Brenda agreed, and gave Joe a warning glance. "No beer. Remember. Not while you're on those pills."

With an irritated cluck, Joe went to the bar where he ordered a gin and tonic for Sheila, a Campari and soda for Brenda and a glass of lemonade for himself.

Waiting for his drinks, he studied the table where Holgate was introducing the two women. Without Sheila and Brenda, he counted ten people around the table.

"Ten little ex-pats sitting out to dine." He grinned to himself. "Wonder which one will choke himself and leave only nine."

"Señor?"

Joe snapped out of his little reverie to find Juan stood close by, one eye on the level of smoke coming from his barbecue.

"Sorry, son. Just looking at the crowd we've just been invited to join, and I was thinking out loud."

Juan followed Joe's gaze. "Ah. Little England."

Joe laughed. "You don't care for them."

"Most of the holiday guests, señor, they are English too, and they are fine. But this group, they are permanent. Residents. Si? They are, how do you say, a different breed."

"You resent them?"

"No, señor, not resent. But they give me and my cleaners

more complaints than all the others. Everything it has to be just so for them."

"Well, Juan, not to worry. I may be able to ruffle a few feathers this week."

"Señor?"

Joe paid for his drinks. "If they're all like Holgate, then I don't like 'em either, and I haven't even met them yet."

A soft breeze from the sea tickled Joe's skin and relaxed him as he crossed the paved area onto the lawns. The coarse grass felt good under his trainers, the unflagging sunshine warmed him, put him at his ease, and the prospect of irritating Holgate cheered him up.

"Someone has to pay for stopping smoking," he muttered to himself.

Putting drinks down before his companions, he slotted into a vacant chair alongside Sheila on his right, and an overweight, elderly woman to his left who was poring over a crossword in one of the broadsheets.

"Now let me see," said Holgate. "Everyone, this is Mo Murray, here with his companions from the north of England. Murray, let me quickly introduce everyone. The Keeligans, the Acres, the Reverend Olivant and his lady wife, Ian Dimmock and his partner, Sandra Greenwood, and Ann Bamford, and not forgetting the lady who keeps us all in check ..." Holgate gestured at the woman sat alongside Joe, who looked up from her crossword and smiled. "Rita Shepperton."

Joe nodded to the people as Holgate ran around the table, and shook hands with one half of the Keeligans, a middle-aged man with straw hair beneath his broad-brimmed, white hat. Alongside Keeligan, his wife sat almost immobile in an electric wheelchair. Ann Bamford also leaned over to shake his hand. A woman in her early forties, according to Joe's estimate, she was shapely, slender and attractive.

"Pleased to meet you, Mo."

"Actually, it's Joe."

Ann laughed. "Oops. Sorry. I should know better than to rely on the Colonel's hearing." She leaned close to Joe, filling his nostrils with expensive perfume. "Between you, me and the gatepost, he's as deaf as the gatepost."

"I'd noticed," Joe replied, and sat down.

"I seem to recall Les Tanner mentioning a chap called Murray," Olivant said. "A restaurateur, I believe."

Joe laughed. "Restaurateur? I always figured Les as an idiot, but never a social climber. I own a trucker's café in Sanford."

"And he makes a bloody fortune," Brenda commented.

Joe guessed that her comment was prompted by what he (and she) sensed as a ripple of disdain run round the table following Joe's description of the Lazy Luncheonette.

Maurice Keeligan was one of a few exceptions. "A truck stop, eh? What's it called? Maybe I dropped in there now and then."

"Used to be Joe's Café," Joe said, "but now it's the Lazy Luncheonette. You were a trucker, Maurice?"

"Had a couple rigs of my own. Sold them for a ridiculous sum about five years ago, when Josie—" he nodded at his disabled wife, "— began to get really ill."

He had a trucker's build about him, too, Joe thought. In his late fifties, not too tall, stocky, with a spreading waistline. Alongside him, Josie could have been younger or older. Slender to the point of emaciation, her fingers curled into unmanageable fists, and her face was lined with the combined effects of pain and too much sun.

She noticed Joe looking and smiled. "Arthritis. Crippling."

"Forgive me," Joe said. "I didn't mean to stare."

"I'm quite used to it, Mr Murray."

Alongside Josie, Ann Bamford stepped in to repeal any embarrassment. "Never thought of investing in property out here, Joe?"

"So I can give my friends and relations free holidays? Not likely. I usually stick to Scarborough and I was surprised when

I found out Les Tanner said he had a place here."

"Been a holiday resident for about five years now, your Mr Tanner," Michael Acre said. "Enjoys comparing notes with the colonel on military matters."

Joe refrained from mentioning that Les Tanner was a part time soldier only. "Are you all permanent residents?"

"All of us. The colonel has been here the longest, followed by Rita." He nodded towards the large woman sat on Joe's left. "The rest of us moved in here over the last two to three years. We're all on level seven, which is why the staff know it as Little England."

"And the rest of the block is bog standard holiday accommodation?" Joe asked.

"All of it is," Acre replied. "Your friend rents out his apartment, but not through an agency. That way he knows who's staying there. The rest of the place is filled with holidaymakers from all over Europe."

Joe smiled broadly and echoed Holgate's earlier comment. "But no riff-raff on level seven?"

"Precisely," Acre said, much to Joe's surprise.

"I was joking."

"I'm not."

Joe could feel his irritation rising, but was saved by the intervention of Juan rattling a dinner gong.

Crowds descended on the barbecue like locusts. To Joe's surprise, Maurice Keeligan even pushed his wife, Josie, along to the serving line. On Sheila's hint, Joe sat it out along with Rita.

She inked in a couple more answers on her crossword, put it down, and said, "Are you not eating, Mr Murray?"

"Mrs Jump and Mrs Riley will sort me out," he told her. "What about you?"

"The colonel knows what I like." Rita leaned into him slightly. "You must know each other very well, you and your lady friends."

He got the feeling Rita was fishing for information rather

than simply being polite, and he recalled George's warning about a 'Rita Shipstone'.

"They work for me," he explained, and rapidly changed the subject. "I must say, I'm surprised to find so many English people living so close together. And you're not all over retirement age, are you?"

"Well, I'm retired, of course. I was a journalist. I worked on some of the country's largest broadsheets. *The Times* and *The Telegraph*, as well as a few regional newspapers." She picked up her newspaper again. "Pass my time doing crosswords. The tougher ones. You know." In an effort to either impress Joe or establish her intellectual superiority over him, she made it sound as if she were ready to accept an award. "The colonel, now, he's retired, too. The Keeligans are, sort of retired. Josie is so ill, you know, and he doesn't trust anyone to look after her. Dimmock, Greenwood and Bamford, they all still work. I think Dimmock works from his apartment. I see him jogging every morning, but I never see him go to an office or anything. Bamford is a saleswoman. Timeshare."

Once more, her tone made it sound as if working for a living was contemptuous, and Joe noticed the way her mention of the names omitted the polite 'Mr', 'Ms' or 'Mrs'.

While Joe worked on a response, Rita took out her mobile telephone, and punched a number in. A moment later, she was talking to Holgate, reminding him that she preferred her burger well done.

Joe guessed the gesture was for his benefit, designed to show the closeness of the residents' community by possession of each other's phone numbers, and her superiority within that clique.

"As a long term resident, you must know the best places to eat and drink round here," he said as she put the phone away.

"The best little restaurant in this part of town is Chico's. The colonel takes his morning coffee there every day at about ten o'clock. The rest of them are more likely to be found in a burger bar. You can't miss it. It's just along the seafront." Rita

35

pointed down to the promenade, and away to their left.

"Good meals?"

Rita laughed falsely. "Oh dear me, I couldn't say, and I'm sure Colonel Holgate can't either. It's far too expensive for poor pensioners like us to dine there. But you young people always have plenty of money, don't you?"

Again, Joe felt she was seeking information, and he wondered whether he was simply biased by the tale and warning George had given him. "How about night life?" he asked.

"You have to go up into town for the clubs and whatnot," Rita told him, "but if you want a lively, English night, there's a bar called Coyote's. Easy to find. Leave the building by the front entrance, turn left up the street and it's the last building on the right. It's not far to walk. Run by Paul and Pauline Wiley. Nice couple."

Joe recalled George recommending it. He also recalled the reason George recommended it, but chose not to say so to Rita. "Why Coyote's? Line dancing or Country and Western, is it?"

Rita laughed and the loose flab on her arms wobbled. "No, no. They're called Wiley. The people who own it. You know. Wile E Coyote. From the cartoons."

"Ah. Right."

Rita returned to her crossword as the rest of the table began to return. Brenda handed Joe a steak sandwich, and a cocktail party atmosphere prevailed, with the regulars regularly swapping seats to chat, politely bringing Joe and his companions into the conversations, sprinkling their chatter with recommendations of the sight the three newcomers should take in.

Over the course of the next hour, Joe found himself in conversation with most of the residents, his attentive ear tuned to slight hints of discontent almost buried in the deluge of banter.

"Rita tells me you're still working," he said to Dimmock.

"Good job she doesn't work for MI5, isn't it? She has no conception of confidentiality." Dimmock scowled in Rita's direction."Like you, I'm a businessman. Investment advisor. I work from the apartment most of the time. On the internet, you know."

Aged about fifty, at the side of Joe he was a huge man, standing well over six feet, with arms like most men's calves. Dark haired, blue-eyed and bronzed, he was the kind of man Brenda liked, but he had already given polite 'not interested' signals to her.

"Paying game," Joe speculated. "I thought you guys made a fortune."

"Not so you notice." Dimmock laughed. "To be honest, Murray, I'm having my own place built on the outskirts of Marbella. Apartmentos Ingles is a stopgap. Useful, economical, but hardly the lap of luxury. He dipped into the back pocket of his shorts and came out with a wallet and handed Joe a business card. "If you have money you'd like to invest, give me call."

"Thanks, but I won't be moving to Spain."

"Internet. Remember? Doesn't matter where you live, I can help." Dimmock cast a sneering glance in Holgate's direction. "He's never even heard of the web. Are you a dinosaur, too?"

"I'm quite good with the web," Joe replied, as Rita glared at Dimmock.

"You shouldn't be so catty, Ian," Rita said. "The colonel may be old fashioned, but we can't fault his values or his organisational abilities."

"Well, you'd know," Dimmock said and wandered off to find fresh conversation.

Rita sighed. "Younger people can be so difficult, Mr Murray."

"I'd hardly describe him as young."

***

With the time coming up to four, and the end of siesta approaching, Joe, Sheila and Brenda excused themselves, made their way down to the seafront, turned left and ambled along the promenade towards the shopping.

"A pleasant lot of people," Sheila commented on their recent company.

Brenda was not so sure. "An undertone, though. Some resentment among a few of them."

Joe was not surprised that Brenda had spotted it. She had always been the more perspicacious when it came to picking up hints. "You noticed it, too? Dimmock doesn't like Holgate."

"The Reverend Olivant isn't too keen on him, either," Brenda reported, "and I'm not too keen on the Reverend Olivant. He kept looking down my cleavage."

"Then cover it up, dear," Sheila suggested.

Joe could not resist poking fun at Brenda. "Not something that normally troubles you, anyway."

"Bog off."

Where the leisure area ended and the shopping area began, heralded by a parade of seafront shops and restaurants, they came upon a sand sculptor working diligently on his latest creation, a large mosque, complete with giant dome, and towers topped by minarets. Wetting his hands in a bucket, he smoothed out a mound of sand, melding it expertly into the overall construction.

"Clever man," Sheila said, taking a photograph while Joe and Brenda dropped coins in a cloth cap on the wall.

Little further along, they found Chico's, a double fronted café/bar/restaurant, most of it outside tables taken up with patrons enjoying the sun, while further back, the interior was almost barren. Joe took in the tariff, emblazoned on several boards outside, and watched a brace of waiters rushing hither and thither to take and fulfil orders, clear away crockery and cutlery and clean ashtrays.

"Looks ideal," Sheila said.

"Dinner tonight then?" Joe asked, his eye on the ashtrays, his thoughts on the luxurious bite of cigarette smoke in his lungs.

"And then that pub Rita Shepperton told you about?" Brenda asked as they moved on.

"Coyote's? Fine."

Sheila noticed Joe's distracted air. "Is there something wrong?"

"Apart from my gasping for a smoke? No. Not really."

"Think of something else," Brenda suggested.

"Think of living here in this glorious weather for the rest of your life."

"Or think of that girl topless sunbathing." Brenda grinned and nodded to the beach.

Joe snapped his head to the right, and scanned the crowd of sun-worshippers on the sands. As usual they came in all shapes and sizes, from the muscular and curvaceous, to the overweight and downright ghastly.

"I can't see any girl topless sunbathing."

"Took your mind off cigarettes for a minute, though, didn't it?"

They passed another pair of illegal traders arguing with a shopkeeper, and although the verbal exchange was carried out in rapid Spanish, Joe needed no translation to work out what was going on. The shopkeeper sold bags, purses and other leather goods, and the traders were displaying similar wares on the ground. He caught the word *policia* amongst the babble, and the grumbling Africans began to pack up their wares, wrapping them in the ground sheets, preparing to move on.

As they came towards the far end of the promenade, where a high and rocky promontory jutted out into the sea, its craggy sides hidden behind a huge holiday complex, they stopped for coffee, attracted by the Union flag outside a bar name Jack &

Jill's. The proprietor, a homely and middle-aged woman who originally came from somewhere in Essex, was pleased to see and serve them, complaining that it had been quiet for most of the day.

"Not the only thing that's been quiet," Brenda commented when the hostess returned to her bar. "You're very pensive, Joe."

"Rita Shepperton," he said.

"Not like you to let people get on your nerves," Sheila observed.

"She isn't … well, she is, but not in the way you think. No, it's something George told me at the Miner's Arms last week."

While they drank coffee, he reiterated the tale. Sheila disapproved, but it came as no surprise to Brenda.

"That's George all over. And the woman he trapped off with runs Coyote's?"

"You're missing the point," Joe said as they left Jack & Jill's and made their way into the busy, narrow backstreets. "It was the way Rita spoke to me earlier. Almost as if she was digging for information."

"Well if she's going to blackmail you, Joe, she'll have to dig very deeply," Sheila said, looking one way and then the other along the street. "You're like me. Very boring."

The street, narrow, composed of high buildings on either side, which blocked out the afternoon sun, was lined with shops on both sides. Shoes, clothing, accessories, souvenirs, and along on the left, a tobacconist's, plied their trade and with siesta time over, they were as busy as any High Street in Great Britain.

"I do not have a boring life," Joe protested as the women made for a shoe shop.

"You don't have a particularly risqué one, either, Joe," Brenda said. "You're not worth blackmailing."

"No, but you might be. Just be careful what you say to Rita Shepperton."

"We're going in here, Joe," Sheila called out as she made her way into the shoe shop. "We'll catch you up.

"And hey," Brenda warned, "keep away from the tobacconist."

Joe waved them irritably away and headed for the tobacconist.

Chapter Four

Returning to Apartmentos Ingles, they showered, changed, and by six thirty they were back at Chico's where they enjoyed an excellent dinner. Joe found his steak done perfectly, Sheila complimented the waiter on her chicken, and the slightly more adventurous Brenda, raved about the paella.

An hour later, they walked back, cut through from the bottom gate of Apartmentos Ingles and, leaving via the main entrance, emerged onto the top street and turned left as they had been directed to walk slowly up the hill.

All three found it hard going in the early evening heat, and even Joe, normally able to handle the extra exertion, complained that it was tiring.

"It's been a long day," he said as they paused to take in a souvenir shop.

Joe picked up a couple of postcards (one for Lee and Cheryl, the other for the 3rd Age Club) and waited outside for his companions.

The side of the street on which the shop stood, the beach side, was lined with the tower blocks of hotels, the same ones as could be seen from the seafront, a hundred metres behind the shop. The opposite side sported a line of bars, a couple of Irish pubs, and a row of restaurants, English, Chinese and German, all clamouring for the attention of holidaymaker and resident alike. So early in the evening, there were few potential customers out, and the greeters, those men and women whose task it was to intercept evening strollers and invite them to dine, looked restless and bored.

"I've often wondered whether it would be worth putting one of you out on Doncaster Road to pull the punters in," Joe said as the women emerged and they resumed their walk up the hill.

"We're a truck stop, not a restaurant, Joe," Sheila reminded him. "What are we going to do? Flag them down as they trundle along the road?"

"We could get Brenda to give them a flash of stocking top," Joe chuckled.

Brenda wafted a newly bought, lace fan before her face. "If you think I'm standing on Doncaster Road wearing a miniskirt and stockings in the middle of winter, you've another think coming, Joe Murray." She grinned cheekily. "Besides, flash my legs at them, and there'd be a string of accidents with all the distracted drivers."

"Modesty becomes you, dear," Sheila chuckled.

A hundred metres further on, the road turned sharply to the right, but straight ahead was a small cul-de-sac, with a turning area large enough for a people carrier or small bus. The entrance to a large hotel lay to the left, and opposite, sited next door to a supermarket proclaiming, *Top British Foods*, was Coyote's.

It was the last building on the right, as they had been told. A three-storey, adobe style place, the entire ground floor spread comprising the bar/restaurant. Joe imagined that the owners lived in the apartments above the pub, just as he lived in the flat above the Lazy Luncheonette.

Thoughts of his business led him to comparisons. Coyote's had a similar spread to the Lazy Luncheonette, but the resemblance ended there. Coyote's enjoyed a range of tables outside on the flagged forecourt. The pavement outside the Lazy Luncheonette was not wide enough for such amenities and even if it were, the British weather would rarely tempt people to eat in the open air. Inside the Lazy Luncheonette the dining area was fairly cramped, seating four to a table on either side of a central aisle of tables which seated eight. The spread inside Coyote's was much freer, more relaxed and airy, tables for four set around the walls, with one or two in the centre, and leaving a gap for karaoke, while the bar was ranged along the back of the room.

The walls, too, were better decorated, covered in photographs of football grounds and teams from the English Premier League. Joe had a large screen TV on one wall, and a range of his casebooks on short shelves.

"I cater for truckers, not holidaymakers," he told Sheila when she marvelled at the difference between the two establishments. "Get 'em in, get 'em fed and get 'em out to make room for the next lot."

They chose a table outside, where they could take in the last of the evening sun. While the women sat, Joe entered the bar.

The pub was already busy, some taking a meal with their drinks, others racking up empty glasses, determined, so it seemed to Joe, to get drunk as quickly as possible. A young man and a boy, who Joe took to be the man's son, were playing pool, others sat around chatting or watching a re-run of *You've Been Framed* on one of four screens hung about the walls, while behind the bar, the staff idled away the minutes, waiting, presumably, for the big rush.

A chunky woman of about fifty greeted him with a broad smile. "Nah then, what can I do you for?"

Joe returned the smile. "That's a grand accent, that it. Wakefield?"

"Not far," she replied. "Morley."

"I'm from Sanford."

"Small world. Or happen not, considering the number of Brits who come here. What y'aving?"

Joe ordered a half of John Smith's bitter for himself, a gin and tonic for Sheila and Campari and soda for Brenda.

While the barmaid prepared the drinks, Joe took in her dark-haired tanned features and as much of the rest of her as he could see. Stocky, a little overweight, but not unlovely, her fingers were adorned with gold and silver. Lively, dark brown eyes darted around the room, and as she worked, her fine fingers tapping the cash register keys as she racked up the drinks, a pleasant smile played about her lips.

She placed the drinks before him. "Nine fifty for cash."

He handed her a ten. "Put the rest in the kitty," he said. "I'll bet you're Pauline."

"Spot on. Pauline Wiley. I own the place. Well, I own it with old misery guts."

Joe raised his eyebrows. "Your better half?"

"My *lesser* half," she corrected him. "Staying at Apartmentos Ingles, are you?"

Joe was impressed. "How did you guess?"

"You knew my name. Most of the Little England crowd come in here. Tom Holgate, Maurice Keeligan, the Olivants, Dimmock and his bint. And that old sow, Rita Shepperton."

Joe laughed. "Joe Murray. I run the Lazy Luncheonette if you're ever in Sanford. We only just got here today, and I'm pleased to say I had 'em sussed dead right. To be honest, it wasn't them who told me your name, but a mate of mine, back home. George Robson. He was here sometime last year."

"Can't say I remember … Oh, wait a minute." Pauline's eye lit up. "Big, strapping lad. Gardener for the local council or summat."

"That's George."

Pauline's smile became slightly more wistful and her eyes gleamed. "Oh, I remember George all right. Is he with you?"

Joe thought he detected more than a note of hope in her voice. "He's in England, digging his gardens or whatever it is he does. I'm here with a couple of friends. Doctor's orders." Picking up his drinks, he winked at her. "I'm outside if you fancy a natter with a few Yorkies when you're on a break."

"Count on it."

Joe ambled back out into the sunset and joined his

companions.

"Should you be having beer?" Sheila asked. "Those painkillers you're taking are quite strong, you know, and it won't mix well with the antibiotics."

"I can handle it," he replied and took a sip of the foaming bitter. "Excellent." He took in their suspicious stares. "Come on, you told me to relax. What better way than sitting in the Mediterranean sun and drinking a decent beer?"

As the sun dipped behind a clutch of trees fronting a low-rise hotel, lights came on and the pub began to fill, until by 8.45, it was quite busy.

Looking down the street, Joe spotted Colonel Holgate and Rita Shepperton making their slow way up the hill, the colonel dressed in his light coloured suit and Panama hat, Rita wearing a loose shawl over a pale blue dress. Not far behind them were Ian Dimmock and Sandra Greenwood, accompanied by Maurice Keeligan and his wife, whose electric wheelchair wobbled erratically from side to side as she struggled to steady the control stick.

When they arrived, they invited themselves to join the three companions, dragging other tables and chairs together so they could sit. Keeligan slotted his wife between Sheila and Brenda, the three men sat opposite Joe, who found himself with Rita and her ubiquitous crossword for company. The colonel placed their order with an arrogant air of authority which would brook no mistakes, and soon, the group melded into disparate but convivial conversations. Sheila and Brenda chatted amiably with Josie and Sandra, Holgate and Dimmock were talking about stock market movements, and Joe found himself in conversation with Rita and Maurice Keeligan, who, from across the table, suggested places to visit.

"If you do get into the town, you must see the church of San Miguel," Rita urged Joe. "Fairly modern, but a pretty little church right at the bottom of Calle San Miguel."

"But watch out for the Olivants," Keeligan chuckled. "They

go there regularly to pray."

"There's nothing wrong with faith, Maurice." Rita scowled at him, then beamed upon Joe. "The Reverend and Mrs Olivant meet with some Christian friends at a café on the Calle San Miguel, quite near the church, and Mr and Mrs Acre enjoy the flamenco and the company at *Bodega Costa del Sol* most afternoons." She nodded towards Sheila and Brenda. "I'm sure your lady friends will love the shopping on Calle San Miguel. It's quite cosmopolitan."

"We can forget fancy words like cosmopolitan where Sheila and Brenda are concerned," Joe grinned. "The word 'shopping' is enough for them."

"They have you well trained, eh, Joe?" Keeligan laughed.

"They think my credit card is a bottomless pit."

Just after ten o'clock, a large, slightly overweight man, his hair thinning, took centre stage by the pool table in the bar, and announced the karaoke.

Looking through the windowless hatch behind their table, Joe watched the first singer give a creditable rendition of Bobby Darin's *Mack The Knife*. A sixty-something from Manchester, he wore a flat cap and slender glasses, dressed in a white, short-sleeved shirt with beer stains down the front, and a pair of baggy denim shorts, which hugged his distended belly at the top and showed his battered, arthritic knees lower down.

"Thank you, Dave from Manchester," said the host when the singer returned to his table. "I was gonna sing the next song myself, so I asked the missus what I should sing and she said, 'Anything but *Sweet Caroline* cos that's me favourite'."

The gag, which Joe reckoned was older than the Lazy Luncheonette, raised a chuckle amongst the busy crowd both inside and out. Excusing himself, Joe left his seat and visited the gents. On his way back out, he caught sight of Pauline Wiley, stood outside, away from the tables, enjoying a smoke, and joined her.

"No smoking inside?" Joe asked.

"The ban's only recently come to Spain," Pauline agreed. "You've had it for years in England, haven't you?"

Joe nodded. "Two thousand and seven, if I remember. It's a bugger. I own a café in Sanford, and I'm not allowed to smoke on my own premises."

"You're preaching to the choir." She took out her pack and offered him one.

Joe was sorely tempted, but declined. "I've had to give it up." He sniffed in a lungful of air. "I'll settle for a bit of passive."

Pauline laughed and Joe glanced back into the bar, where the host, obviously short of volunteers, was now singing *Candle In The Wind.*

"He your regular host, is he? Only his jokes are older than me."

"That's my husband, Paul," Pauline told him.

Joe grimaced. "Sorry."

"No. You're right. His jokes are from the back page of the Dandy." Pauline laughed, then suddenly became more serious. "Listen, Joe, I don't know what George told you about last year, but—"

"He told me," Joe interrupted. "It's bog standard George, and nothing to do with me, Pauline. I don't sit in judgement on anyone."

She crushed out her cigarette on the ground, and tapped the side of her nose. "Not a word to the old man, eh?"

Joe smiled. "You can count on my discretion."

Pauline returned to the bar, Joe looked up into the sky at the first stars twinkling in the dark, and turned to go back to the table, only to find himself confronted with Rita Shepperton.

"Beautiful part of the world, here, you know, Joe," she said, gazing up into the sky. "You don't mind if I call you Joe, do you?"

"It is my name, and it's better than the names some people call me."

"You know Pauline, do you? From England?"

"Never met her before, but she comes from a little town just outside Leeds, and so do we."

"I remember you telling me. Do you know the man she had a bit of a fling with last year? What was his name, now? George something or other." Rita put on a convincing impression of someone struggling to recall a name. "Anyway, he came from Sanford, too. He was another friend of Captain Tanner and Mrs Goodson."

"I know George, yes." Joe waited to see where the conversation was going.

"He didn't waste any time getting his feet under Pauline's table, if you see what I mean."

"That sounds like George," Joe agreed, and remained silent again.

"Small town, Sanford, isn't it?"

"Are you trying to say something, Rita?" Joe asked. "Sanford is a small town, yes, and we have this awful habit of just saying what we think."

"Really? How quaint." She gripped his arm in a gesture of intimacy that Joe did not like. "I was just thinking how terrible it would be if Mr Riley and Mr Jump learn that their wives had been on holiday with another man."

Joe suppressed the urge to burst out laughing. "I think it would be, er, very surprising."

"Small town like Sanford. Wouldn't take long to track them down, would it?"

"No, it wouldn't," Joe replied.

"So how much do you think it would be worth to make sure they don't find out? A hundred euros, perhaps?"

Joe could hold himself no longer. He laughed aloud. Controlling his mirth and keeping his voice down, he said, "Tell you what, Rita, why don't you take your offer and stick it where the sun don't shine? And if you want to track down Colin Jump and Peter Riley, I'd suggest you start with Sanford

Crematorium. I'm sure there are plaques for both men."

Leaving her gawping in embarrassment, he yanked his arm free of her grip and made his way back to the table.

***

It was turned midnight before they left Coyote's, and by then Joe had had another three drinks.

On the walk back to Apartmentos Ingles, he told them of his brief encounter with Rita Shepperton, and concluded, "George was right about her. He said she tried to nail him for a hundred euros. Blackmailing old sow."

"No blackmailer would be that transparent, Joe," Brenda told him. "She's probably short of money and trying to make a few bob."

"Not out of me, she doesn't."

Once back at the apartment, Joe, feeling the pain of his left arm, settled on the balcony with a cup of tea and his pills, to the concern of the two women.

"You shouldn't be taking those on top of beer," Sheila reproved.

"I can cope with it," he said as he sat on the balcony with his companions, enjoying a final cup of tea. He swallowed two painkillers and sat back, staring out to sea, contented. "It's been a good day."

In the distance the lights of Malaga gleamed through the night. The stars shone in an ink black sky, and out to sea a line of bright, white lights were strung across the sea, stretching for as far they could see in both directions.

"Night fishing," Brenda said.

"You've seen it before?" Sheila asked.

"Colin and I stayed on a holiday complex further down the coast, between Marbella and Estepona." Brenda yawned. "It must be, oh, twenty-five years or more now. I remember thinking what a beautiful sight, all those little lights on the sea, like illuminations."

Joe found her yawn infectious. "Yeah, well, it's been a long day. Time I was giving out some zeds, I think." He stood up and swayed against the wall.

"Steady, Joe. Don't want you going over the balcony."

"Just a bit, er, you know ... tired."

"Too much beer and pills."

"And a slack of leep ... I mean lack of ... y'know. I'll see you tomorrow."

He wove his way into the apartment, and through to his room. Throwing off his clothing, he climbed into bed and minutes later he was asleep ...

"I'm telling ... she won't stand for it ... we'll ... of something else."

The noise of a man's voice coming into the room from a somewhere along the landing woke Joe.

Bleary eyed and woozy, he glanced at his watch, its luminous dial reading a minute or two after five.

A second voice, also male, reached him. "... Stop griping and ..."

Joe threw off the single sheet, determined to give the two men a piece of his mind. He sat up, the room span, and he laid his head back on the pillow, closing his eyes to the night, his ears to the argument.

***

A dazzling bead of incandescent scarlet broke the horizon and Joe snapped the shutter of his Sony camera.

Satisfied with the picture of the first rays of the sun above the sea, bringing with it the promise of another hot day, he placed the camera carefully on the balcony table, and patted his pockets, seeking his tobacco. With some frustration he recalled he was now a non-smoker.

"I'm gasping, too," he told himself.

He needed something to take his mind off smoking, but at eight fifteen in the morning, there was precious little in the way of distractions. Seated with his back to the wall, away from the balcony rail, he could just see the beach and promenade. The sands were deserted, and few people were visible on the promenade, where a small road sweeper made its way along, clearing up the detritus of the previous day. The cafés and shops would not open for another forty-five minutes or more, and Torremolinos in general would not come properly alive until getting on for ten o'clock.

Out to sea there wasn't much more going on. The dotted lamps of the previous night's fishing boats were gone. A small boat chugged out of Benalmedina, travelling northeast towards Malaga, and in the far distance, he could make out the tiny lights of a larger ship.

He had slept well. Aside from the single disturbance at five o'clock, he had not woken, but he was still out of bed at just after six, which he reasoned, was the same as five in Sanford, the time he got up every day of the week. But he felt light-headed, and he realised the inadvisability of drinking beer while taking painkillers and antibiotics. It was not, he vowed, a mistake he would repeat.

Stepping out onto the balcony with a cup of tea, he had learned that at such an early hour, the grounds of Apartmentos Ingles were in total darkness. He could see the outlines of chairs and tables, and the swimming pool, with a large inflatable floating on its still surface. Now with the sun rising the dawn flooded the beach and promenade with light. In the distance, through the early mist, sunlight glittered from what Joe imagined was a high rise building in Malaga, and bounced back to dazzle him, and an aircraft approaching the airport glistened in the early light.

And with it all, came the same sense of peace he had had the previous day when he first looked out from the balcony. Exactly the kind of peace and relaxation McKay had ordered.

The rattle of cup and saucer from the kitchen told him one of his companions was also up and about.

"Good morning, Joe. Enjoying the view?"

"Morning, Sheila. Yes. Taking it easy."

"Would you like a fresh cup?"

"No, thanks. I'm well armed."

He listened to her tinkering and pottering with the kettle and crockery, and it called to mind the Lazy Luncheonette, his little gold mine 1200 miles to the north, where Lee and his wife Cheryl would now be in dealing with the heaviest of the morning trade, the draymen clamouring for food. Joe smiled wryly. Lee and Cheryl could have it. He was not missing it.

"Beautiful morning."

Sheila's comment as she stepped out on the balcony, skirted round him and took a seat on the other side of the table, brought him back from the rain of West Yorkshire to the sun, sand and calm of the Costa del Sol. From beneath them came the sound of one of the cleaners, moving chairs and tables around on the paved patio area by the outside bar, and her constant chatter with a colleague.

Joe listened to it without catching or understanding a word, and mentally compared it with the Lazy Luncheonette where Sheila and Brenda would often gossip while working.

"Sleep well?" he asked.

"Not bad," Sheila replied. "Woke up just once. A loud splash from the pool and a terrible scraping, rattling sound. Younger lads messing about, I imagine."

"Funny that," Joe said. "I got woke up by an argument somewhere on our landing. Five-ish. Bit doped up so I couldn't hear properly."

Sheila smiled. "You didn't go out and give them a piece of the Joe Murray mind?"

"I was going to, but I couldn't be bothered. Besides, you keep telling me we're on holiday. If I get woke in the middle of the night, I've plenty of time to catch up on sleep, haven't I?"

He sipped his tea. "You didn't check on who was messing in the pool?"

Sheila shook her head. "Visited the smallest room, got back into bed and went back to sleep."

Sheila gazed across the sea towards Malaga and sighed contentedly. "How very calm and peaceful."

"My very thoughts just before you came—"

A sharp, high-pitched cry from below cut Joe off.

"*Socorro. Está muerta. ¡Ayúdame!*"

"What the hell—"

Sheila, too, cut Joe off. "*Socorro* means help—"

"I thought you didn't speak Spanish."

"— and *muerta* means …"

As Sheila trailed off, they both leapt for the balcony rails and stared down.

One of the cleaners, obviously distressed, was running from the pool back towards the building. As Joe watched, Juan appeared and stopped the young woman, his hands on her shoulders, urging her to look at him and explain herself.

Joe's gaze shifted to the pool and the large inflatable he had first noticed in the dark. It was not an inflatable. It was the body of an overweight woman, her thin clothing ballooned out around her as she floated face down on the still water.

"Oh my god," Sheila said. "It's Rita Shepperton."

Chapter Five

Joe, out of breath, his heart pumping frenetically, weaved his way through the tables, chairs and loungers dotted about the lawns, skirted the final lounger standing by the edge of the pool, and found Juan, stripped down to his shorts, in the water, swimming across to Rita's body, gingerly reaching out for her.

"What the hell are you doing, man?" Joe asked. "You need to leave her where she is and call the police."

"But she may be alive," Juan protested.

"She's dead. She's been there since six o'clock to my knowledge."

Treading water, Juan looked suspiciously up at him as Ian Dimmock and Maurice Keeligan hurried across the lawns.

"You saw her at six o'clock?" Juan asked. "Yet you did nothing."

"It was dark. I didn't realise it was a body," Joe argued.

"What else could it be, señor?"

"An … er … oh, for crying out loud, stop arguing. Just leave her there, Juan, and get the police out."

"What are you talking about, Murray?" Dimmock asked. "We need to get her out of the water. We may be able to save her."

"She's been in there at least two hours, probably longer," Joe snapped. "You can't move her. The police will need to see the body where and as it is."

"Why?" Keeligan demanded.

"She could have been murdered."

"Don't talk such rubbish," Dimmock said. "She had a weak heart. It's more likely to be a heart attack."

"Get her out of the water," Keeligan urged.

"She's dead and you need to leave her where she is."

Ignoring Joe, Dimmock directed his words at Juan. "Check for a pulse."

"And how do I do that?"

"Her neck," Keeligan urged. "Press your finger against her neck, see if you can feel her heartbeat."

Juan reached tentative fingers out and pressed them to Rita's neck. Almost immediately, her body began to float away. He looked up at them and shrugged.

"Let's get her out," Dimmock suggested. "Pinero, push her to this edge."

"Dimmock, I'm telling you—"

"Just shut up and mind your own business, Murray," Dimmock ordered and moved the nearby lounger away from the poolside, to leave room for Rita's body.

Frustrated but having to back down in the face of Dimmock's assumed authority, Joe glanced up at the building. Many people had come out onto their balconies to see what the fuss was about. On the seventh floor, Sheila and Brenda hung over the rail, their faces etched with concern.

Joe cupped his hands to his mouth, and called out, "Take pictures. My camera."

Dimmock scowled. "Are you some kind of ghoul?"

"No," Joe snapped. "An experienced detective."

***

On the balcony of apartment 705, Brenda watched the scene with dismay. "This is the worst thing that could have happened."

"The poor woman," Sheila simpered.

"I didn't mean her. I meant Joe."

56

Sheila whirled her head round. "What on earth are you talking about, Brenda?"

"Think about it, Sheila. Joe has had some kind of … I don't know … health incident. We came here to relax, unwind him. Now a body's turned up, and we both know Joe. The local police will tell him to mind his own business, and even though he doesn't speak much Spanish, they'll get the message across. But we know Joe. If he sniffs a problem, and he will, he won't be able to keep out of it. It's exactly what he doesn't need."

Sheila nodded and Brenda was satisfied that she had got the message across.

"In that case, we'll need to keep an eye on him."

They returned to watching events below.

Joe signalled to them, cupping his hands to his mouth and shouting something. Brenda cupped a hand to her ear indicating that they could not hear, and Joe imitated a camera.

"He wants us to take a picture?" Brenda was appalled. "What the hell is he—"

"It's not him, it's those idiots," Sheila said, and hurried back into the apartment. She returned a moment later with Joe's camera, switched it on, and put it to her eye. "They're moving the body, the damned fools."

***

Satisfied that Sheila had a photographic record of events, Joe backed off and sat on the lounger Dimmock had moved.

Slowly, and with great respect, her body was manhandled from the water and laid on the pool edge, face up. Joe turned away from the sight of her lifeless, ashen face.

Dimmock knelt and put his ear to her chest. He looked up at Keeligan and shook his head.

"Get some towels," Keeligan said. "Cover her up."

Joe tutted. "You don't listen, do you?"

"Now listen, Murray—"

57

Joe leapt to his feet and interrupted. "No, you listen, Dimmock. How many deaths have you seen? How many have you investigated? I've been in this situation more times than you've had your secretary. I told you she was dead. I didn't recognise her body for what it was in the dark, but I saw her there at six o'clock; two and a half hours ago. She may have had a heart attack, she may have drowned, she may have been murdered, but you've just made the police job that much harder by moving the body, and now you want to cover her. I'm no scientist but that may have an effect on the rate of decomposition and make the pathologist's death so much harder. Now leave her be. Cover her face, if you must, but no more."

The receptionist, Christobel appeared, and addressed the two residents. "I have called the police. They are on their way. They ask that you do not touch anything."

"You're too late," Joe grumbled.

He turned to walk away and as he did, he felt the damp from the seat of his shorts. Puzzled, he turned back and studied the lounger. The blue canvas varied in shade on all the loungers: the effects of age, usage and variable sunlight, he guessed. The one on which he had been sat, however, was much darker than the rest. When he touched it, it wasn't merely damp, but soaking wet.

"Problem, Murray?" Dimmock demanded

"Yeah. This is wet. When we got here it was at the edge of the pool."

"Rita must have been using it," Keeligan said. "Getting ready for her swim."

Joe shook his head. "I said it's wet. Not damp, but soaking. And if she used it to get ready for her swim, it would have been dry."

"And if she dived in, it would have been splashed," Dimmock argued. "Problem solved."

"You think so?"

58

"Seems reasonable to me," Dimmock replied.

Joe glared. "In that case, I take it back. You're not simply lacking in knowledge, you're completely gormless." He stormed away.

Entering the building, he met with Holgate, who asked what was going on. Joe explained and Holgate nodded judiciously.

"Hardly a surprise, I must say."

"How so?" Joe asked.

"Not long since her last heart attack. What? Five, six weeks. Something like that. We didn't get an awful lot of sleep that night, either. And the doctors warned her, you know. Told her to take it easy. But she would have her early morning swim."

"You're telling me she used to swim in the dark?"

Fitting a cigarette into his holder, Holgate nodded. "Not the slimmest or most attractive of women, as I'm sure you noticed. Preferred to swim when others couldn't see her. Knew it would be the end of her one day."

With a stiff nod, Holgate went on his way, out through the front doors, and Joe, his mind ticking over the events of the last half hour, took the lift up to the seventh floor.

***

Joe, Sheila and Brenda were on the balcony, the women leaning on the rail watching events unfold below, Joe making notes on his netbook, when the apartment doorbell rang. Answering it, he met with Juan, now dried off and fully clothed.

"*La Policia* … the police, Señor Murray, they wish to speak with you and your ladies."

Joe nodded. "We'll be right down."

The time was coming up to eleven o'clock. After the initial furore of finding Rita, and the argument over moving her body, with nothing better to do, Joe and his companions had

59

taken a walk along the seafront, where they enjoyed a full English breakfast in Chico's, followed by some souvenir hunting before returning to Apartmentos Ingles.

"The cops will want to speak to us," Joe had assured his friends.

Both women had noticed his sombre, reflective mood over the meal.

"Something's bothering you, Joe," Sheila said. "Rita? Thinking about her and heart attack?"

"Hmm? What? No. Well, not really. I am thinking about Rita, but not about heart attack."

"Joe, you're supposed to be taking it easy here," Brenda said. "Don't go looking for things that aren't there. You'll only wind yourself up."

"You try and stop me," Joe had replied. "Y'see, there's something not right about it. That lounger keeps nagging at me. How could it get so wet? It's as if it had been in the pool."

"Well perhaps it had," Sheila suggested. "That strange scrapping and rattling sound I heard."

"Yeah, and that's what doesn't make sense."

The women raised eyebrows at him, inviting elucidation.

"You heard a splash and the scraping noise, Sheila. If the splash was Rita going into the pool, then who pulled the lounger out?"

"Suppose," Sheila suggested, "the splash wasn't Rita going into the pool, but the lounger? And suppose the scraping sound I heard was her pulling the lounger out again?"

"That kind of exertion could have caused her heart attack," Brenda agreed.

"Then how come Sheila didn't hear a second splash as Rita fell in?"

Brenda considered this. "Well, maybe Rita dragged the lounger out of the pool, sat down for a minute to get her breath back and then had the heart attack. Sheila could have gone back to sleep by then."

"And just maybe someone else was there. Someone who pushed her in, knocked the lounger in by accident and had to drag it out again."

They left the debate there and returned to Apartmentos Ingles, where Joe introduced himself to a police officer, only to be told that Inspector Terrones was interviewing residents and would get to them in due course.

With Juan's call, they made their way down to the pool area and Joe introduced them to the inspector.

A tall, broad-shouldered and muscular man, he was dressed in a uniform of navy blue trouser and crisp, pale blue shirt. Joe felt uncomfortable at the sight of a pistol at Terrones' waist, but the man himself appeared totally at ease, drinking coffee, amiable, dark eyes warm, his seductive, Latino tones both relaxing and reassuring.

"Señor Murray, Señora Riley, Señora Jump, allow me to introduce myself, I am Inspector Terrones of the *Policia Nacional,* the Spanish national police. It is my job to inquire into the death of Rita Shepperton. So …" He gave a casual shrug. "At the moment, we have no evidence of foul play. I understand from Pinero, the janitor, that you were the first person to his aid at the pool this morning."

Joe nodded. "I'd been looking out over the sea from my balcony when I heard him shout for help. I got down here as quick as I could."

"He also says to me that you objected when Señor Dimmock and Señor Keeligan dragged Señora Shepperton from the pool. I am also told that you declared the lady dead. You are a doctor?"

Joe chuckled without humour. "No. Nothing like that. I just have a bit of experience of these things, and I know she was in the water at six this morning. She couldn't have been in there that long and survived. She had to be dead. I did warn them that they shouldn't have moved her. I knew you'd want to see her in situ, as it were." Joe patted his camera. "Mrs Riley did get some photographs, though."

"We will look at them soon. I have spoken to Juan Pinero and Señor Dimmock and Señor Keeligan and told them they should not have moved the body, but I am not too worried by it."

"Really? Only in our country, the cops would be up in arms if anyone moved the body."

"You are a police officer?"

"No. I er …" Joe trailed off wondering best how to explain his role in the many cases he had helped solve. "I have a niece who's a detective sergeant with the police and I'm a sort of a, er private investigator. I help the police now and then."

"I see. I doubt that your assistance will be needed this morning, señor. I have spoken to the staff and Señora Shepperton's neighbours and they tell me that this lady had a heart attack just a few weeks ago. It seems likely that she died of another heart attack. Unless you can say for certain that her death was at the hands of another."

Joe sucked in his breath. "No, no. I can't say that. Not for sure. But …" Again, Joe trailed off.

"You have something to say, Señor Murray?"

"Well, look, this is all a bit hazy, but I got woke up this morning by an argument on our landing."

"Landing?"

"Yes, you know. The floors, the, er, decks." Joe gestured up at the building. "I'm staying with friends, Mrs Riley and Mrs Jump, and my room is on the other side of the building, facing out onto the landings, the decks. Five o'clock this morning, I heard an argument."

"Do you know who was arguing?"

"No. It sounded like two men, and I'm sure one of them said, 'she won't allow it'." Joe shook his head in frustration. "Everything is a bit hazy, y'see. I'm taking these pills. Painkillers and they make me, er, dopey."

"Dazed?" Terrones asked, and Joe nodded. "So you heard an

argument and this was at about five in the morning, but you do not know who was arguing and you do not know what they were arguing about?"

"That's about the size of it."

"You are absolutely certain of the time?"

"I checked my watch." Feeling inadequate, Joe went on hastily, "but my friend, Mrs Riley, heard a splash."

"Very well." Terrones concentrated on Sheila. "Señora?"

Sheila nodded. "Someone or something falling into the pool, and this odd scraping sound immediately after. It was in the early hours. I'd woke up in need of the, er, the smallest room."

"The bathroom?" Terrones asked, and Sheila agreed.

"As I went back into our bedroom, I heard these noises."

"You did not go to the window or the balcony to investigate?"

"No. No, I didn't. I wish I had now, but I just assumed it was someone going for an early morning swim."

"Do you know what time this happened?"

Silently, Joe cursed himself. It was a question he should have asked, but had forgotten.

"About twenty past four."

"You are certain?"

"Oh yes," she replied. "I checked my clock as I went back to bed."

Terrones swung his benign attention back to Joe. "You see, Mr Murray? You heard the argument at five o'clock, yet Mrs Riley, she heard the splash at four twenty. If you are both certain of the time, as you say you are, it is unlikely that the two events are connected."

"Obviously not," Joe said. "So what do you think happened?"

"I can only speculate, señor, and I will have no proper answers until I get an autopsy report, but I believe Mrs Shepperton, she was in the habit of taking an early morning swim, and this morning, the cold of the water produced a heart attack."

"If so, she would still have been breathing, and there will be pool water in her lungs," Sheila pointed out.

"As I said, Señora Riley, I must wait for the pathologist's report."

"And what the hell was she doing swimming fully clothed?" Joe demanded.

Half turning in his seat, Terrones gestured at the sun lounger nearest the pool. "You will notice that the lounger is completely wet. Most of them, they get a spray of water from the sprinkler system, or when people dive into the pool, but that one is properly wet. I think, perhaps, that Mrs Shepperton was, how do you say, skinny dipping. I noticed she wore no underwear beneath her blouse and skirt. She climbed out, dressed and rested on the lounger. The combination of the cold water and exertion brought on a heart attack, and as she tried to get up from the lounger, she died and rolled into the pool."

Joe shook his head in disbelief. "What was the silly old sow doing skinny dipping in the middle of the night?"

Terrones smiled broadly. "We Spanish, we are not so inhibited as you British, but even we do not like the naked swimmers in broad daylight, señor. If you wish to skinny dip, you do it in the dark when no one else can see." The inspector drank off his coffee. "We will make a routine check of her apartment, see to learn if there are relatives we can contact. After that, I think our investigation may be closed. Mr Murray, Mrs Riley, I would like to thank you both for your assistance. If there is anything else that you can think of which may help us to close this file quickly, please get in touch through the reception desk."

Joe and Sheila came away from the table as Terrones began to marshal his officers, barking orders at them in rapid Spanish.

"Poor woman," Sheila said as they rejoined Brenda.

"Yeah. I don't think."

The two women turned on Joe.

"I've heard that tone before, Joe Murray," Brenda said. "I'll not warn you again. You're here for rest and recuperation, not to imagine murders where they don't exist."

"I'm here to be bored out of my skull, you mean. Listen to me, both of you. Terrones knows about her heart condition, and Holgate told me she'd had a heart attack a few weeks ago. She never mentioned it yesterday, did she?"

"Get real, Joe," Brenda laughed. "You wouldn't bring that up in the course of a conversation. Hello, I'm Rita Shepperton and I had a heart attack last month and I could drop dead at any time." She laughed again.

Joe bristled. "That woman was a blackmailer. No, listen to me, cos I'm telling you." He cut off their protests before they could materialise. "She tried her luck with George last year, she tried it with me last night. What price someone decided he – or she – wasn't going to pay and instead made her pay with her life?"

"You don't know that, Joe," Sheila protested. "In fact, you know nothing about the woman."

"Yes I do. I just said, I know she was a blackmailer."

"The stunt she pulled with you and George doesn't make her a blackmailer, Joe," Brenda said. "You make it sound like she was into it big time. I said this last night. She was probably a sad old woman, a bit short of cash, trying to tap you for a hundred euros. She was just testing the waters."

"All right, so she was testing, and she failed. But that doesn't mean she didn't test others and pass."

"Calm down, Joe," Brenda advised. "Even if it were true, there's no way you would ever prove anything. Do like you're supposed to do and take life easy. Read your James Bond book."

"It's Sherlock Holmes."

Brenda smiled. "I knew it was some upper class twit playing the big hero."

Joe shrugged off her light-heartedness. "You two can suit yourselves, I still think this is iffy."

Sheila checked her watch. "Well, why don't you think about it over lunch, Joe? It's getting on for eleven o'clock, and time we were feeding. And then maybe an hour on the beach."

Brenda agreed. "Or a touch of retail therapy."

Joe nodded. "I'll just nip back to the apartment and get my copy of a heroic, upper class twit."

Chapter Six

Arriving on the seventh floor, instead of making his way into their apartment, Joe walked along the landing to Rita Shepperton's where a police officer was applying tape over the door.

The white tape was emblazoned with the words *C. NACIONAL DE POLICIA* in blue, flanked by the warning, *NO PASAR* in red.

Joe needed no translation to tell him that they had sealed the apartment for the time being. With no sign of Terrones, he made his way back to their apartment, picked up his book, and then returned to the ground floor where he met Sheila and Brenda.

"Change of plan," Sheila greeted him with a smile. "Mr Olivant has just told us there's excellent shopping in Benalmedina Harbour, so we're having a wander over there. We'll get to the beach after lunch."

"Are you coming with us, Joe?" Brenda asked. "Or do you want to sit on the sands and we'll find you later?"

"No, no. That's okay. I'll come with you, I'll need souvenirs for Lee and Cheryl, and I want to buy something special for Danny."

Leaving Apartmentos Ingles, they wandered to the bottom of the street where, instead of turning left for Torremolinos, they turned right towards the tiny harbour with its chunky lighthouse on the rocky outcrop.

Apart from the ever-present illegal traders displaying their wares on the ground, the shopping and cafés were rarer here, until they passed the boundary of the two towns, where they came upon a short row of shops.

Joe spent ten minutes in a busy souvenir shop and came out with a new tobacco tin, emblazoned with the legend, Costa del Sol and a cartoon, smiling sun.

"Waste of money, Joe," Brenda declared. "You don't smoke anymore."

"I might start again."

From there, they moved around a hotel complex until they came upon the harbour proper.

Across a wide expanse of car park was a nightclub/casino complex, the building shaped to look like a Mississippi paddle steamer, complete with an entrance that looked like the paddle wheels.

Making their way further round, they came across more shops, alongside the actual marina, and a large apartment complex on the far side. Moorish in design, the apartments, like some of the yachts and boats in the water, stood out like millionaires' playthings.

While Sheila and Brenda disappeared into a clothing shop, Joe secured a table at a café, signalled for service, and studied the various craft in the marina.

They came in many shapes and sizes, from small motor boats, to thirty-foot yachts. Across the other side, he could see much larger launches, the kind usually associated with millionaires.

It was odd how a walk of a few hundred metres could see such a change in fortune. Torremolinos, long recognised as a favourite with the working class families of Great Britain, still had that aura of the holiday brochure about it. Sun, sand and fun. Benalmedina, on the other hand, painted a very different picture. No seafront hotels, and only a few, refined, bars, no karaoke, and the souvenir shops were slightly less 'in your face'.

If he travelled from Sanford to Wakefield, a distance of only a few miles, he would hardly notice the difference. Both were former coal towns, the people were of the same mould, hardy, grafters who complained a lot yet still turned out for their shift. Here, there was an abrupt demarcation, signalled by the marina. Everything to the east was fun loving Torremolinos, everything to the west was the more sober and infinitely wealthier Benalmedina.

"*Si, señor?*"

Joe looked up into the waitress' smiling eyes. "Sorry, luv. I was miles away there. Er, could I have three coffees, please?"

"*Con leche?* Er, weeth—"

"Milk? Yes. Please."

She returned to the café and Joe ruminated once more on the stark difference between this area and the place where they were staying, less than a kilometre to the east. Why, he asked himself, had people like Holgate and the Olivants, and especially Dimmock chosen *Apartmentos Ingles* rather than come to this area. If early impressions were anything to go by, they could easily afford this side of the line, and it would be more in keeping with their self-important attitudes.

He tapped his pockets, found the comfort of his new tobacco tin and was about to take it out when he recalled he was no longer a smoker.

The realisation came as a surprise. Back home, he had sneaked the occasionally cigarette, usually in the privacy of his apartment above the Lazy Luncheonette, or when he was alone in his car. Since their arrival the previous day, the thought of a smoke occurred to him occasionally, but he had now gone almost thirty-six hours without tobacco and aside from moments like this, when he needed to think and the craving threatened to overwhelm him, it had not been a trouble to him.

"Bloody prices," Brenda said, as the two women joined him, bringing him back from his thoughts.

"Sorry? Not like you to moan about such things, Brenda."

"They're average ten percent higher than the shops we

looked at in Torremolinos yesterday," Sheila said.

As the waitress brought their coffee, Joe gestured at the upmarket surroundings. "My guess is rents are probably ten percent dearer down here, too." He cracked a sachet of sugar into his coffee and stirred. "So what do you want to do? Go back to Torremolinos?"

Brenda checked her watch. "Probably a good idea. It's getting on for one o'clock, and I don't know about you two, but I could do with some lunch."

"Forever hungry," Joe said. He picked up the bill. "Mind you. You're probably right. Judging by the price of coffee here. I wouldn't like to pay for …" He trailed off, staring at the time stamp on the bill. "What time did you say it was, Brenda?"

She checked her watch again. "Ten to one."

Sheila checked hers. "I make it just after quarter to."

Joe glanced at his rotary. "You're both wrong. It's quarter to two."

"No, Joe, you're wrong. You're an hour fast."

He shook his head and handed them the bill. "See. The time is on the bottom of the receipt, and my watch is right." The truth slowly dawned on him. "You didn't alter your watches did you? Y'know, when the captain told us that the Costa del Sol is an hour ahead of British time. I altered my watch right away. You never changed yours, did you?" He laughed at them. "And you've the cheek to call me a bloody idiot …" He trailed off again, staring at his watch, his face a mask of intense concentration. "No. It can't be."

"Can't be what, Joe?" Sheila asked.

"You couldn't have made such an elementary mistake."

"What?" Brenda urged. "Joe, what are you talking about?"

He faced them with greater urgency. "Your clock? Did you change it?"

"It's battery operated, Joe," Sheila explained. "I left the battery out while we were travelling. I didn't need to change it because it wasn't working."

"So how and when did you set it?"

"Last night as we were going to bed."

"And you set it by your watch. Right?" Joe waited for her to nod. "So your clock is an hour slow, too."

Brenda took umbrage. "All right, Joe. There's no need to rub it in. It's not the end of the world."

"Don't you see?" Joe again urged them to understand. "I heard an argument at five o'clock. But I altered my watch on the plane when the pilot told us, so it was telling me the right, local time. You heard a splash at twenty past four this morning, but it wasn't twenty past four, because you'd set your clock to BST, the same as your watch. It was twenty past five. The splash followed the argument, not the other way round. That puts a whole new perspective on things."

"How so?" Brenda asked.

"I can see what Joe is saying," Sheila said. "According to us, there was a splash at twenty past four and Joe heard an argument forty minutes later. Inspector Terrones said they would be unlikely to be connected, and you have to agree. If we assume the splash was Rita going into the pool, then the argument came after she died. But in reality, there was an argument and Rita died *after* it. I repeat: if we assume the splash was her body going into the pool."

"Correct," Joe said. "Now think about what I heard. I was doped up on those painkillers, but I'm sure it was two men, and one said to the other, 'she won't stand for it' and the other said, 'stop griping'. Let's stretch our imagination a bit, huh? Let's imagine they were two of Rita's blackmail victims—"

Brenda interrupted him. "Joe, we said earlier, we don't know that Rita was a blackmailer."

"I said we were stretching our imagination. You might not think she was, but I'm certain of it. So let's say the two men were victims, and let's imagine one of them has come up with an idea for warning her off or knocking down the price of her demands. They're nervous about approaching her, and the other is saying she won't stand for it. They go to see her, there's an argument, they knock her cold, and decide they're gonna deal with her permanently. So they haul her down to the pool, chuck her in and leave her there. Twenty minutes between the argument and the splash would be about right. The time it takes to get her from her apartment, down to the pool and drop her in."

"Terrones said she didn't drown, Joe," Sheila pointed out.

"He actually said he wouldn't know until they get the post-mortem report," Joe countered.

"And the curious scraping noises I heard?" Sheila pressed, battering at Joe's arguments.

"Easy. You noticed the lounger by the pool was soaking wet? Terrones speculated that Rita had had a swim and lay down on it for a few minutes before the heart attack. I'm thinking the killers rested Rita's body on it, then tipped her into the pool, but they let go of it and the lounger slipped in. The scraping you heard was the silly sods pulling the lounger back out of the pool."

"But surely it would have dried out by the time Rita's body was discovered."

Joe shook his head. "The sun would dry it out eventually, but the sun doesn't come up until twenty past eight. The maid was screaming for help just after sunrise. It hadn't had chance to dry out."

Brenda drank her coffee. "All right. If we accept what you're saying, Joe, what do we do next?"

"We need to speak to Terrones again. I really should have come clean with him this morning and told him what she tried to pull on me yesterday, and what she tried with George when he was here last year. If we get a move on, he may still be at the Apartmentos Ingles."

Joe left the money for the bill, and they walked out of the café, back onto the marina quayside.

"Suspects?" Sheila asked.

"I spoke to Rita yesterday, she wasn't very complimentary about her neighbours, so it could be any of them. My money would be on Maurice Keeligan and Ian Dimmock."

"Why?" Brenda asked, her eyes roaming over a gleaming white motor launch where a deck hand, stripped to the waist, was polishing the chrome rails, his finely toned muscles glistening in the early afternoon sun.

"They're the youngest, fittest and most muscular," Joe said, also looking the young man over. "And I'd have thought you'd twig that before anyone, Brenda."

Regardless of Joe's sense of urgency, the walk back to Apartmentos Ingles was no faster than the journey to Benalmedina. His two companions paused to look in shop windows, admiring clothing and accessories, and they spent a good ten minute in a shoe shop trying on various items of footwear before coming out empty-handed. Coming back towards the boundary between the two towns, they paused for a rest and ice cream to ward off the heat in this hottest part of the day, and Joe complained that he was gasping for a cigarette.

"Resist, Joe," Sheila advised. "A few more days and you'll get over the cravings and you'll feel like a new man."

"Not literally, I hope," Joe grumbled. "Brenda's the one who feels like a new man … about every three months."

Sheila giggled and the victim of this badinage took it in good part.

"There's so much you'd be able to do for me, Joe, if you were a non-smoker and if you didn't have a weak heart."

Joe did not take the jibe as kindly as Brenda had taken his. "I do not have a weak heart. Just a pulled muscle. And pain. Lots of pain. Pain in the arm and two pains in the—"

"Don't push your luck, Joe," Sheila interrupted.

They moved on.

Sheila paused by the display from a painter, his paintings standing on the low wall of the promenade. Each was a landscape, which Joe assumed was a view from somewhere both local and rural, but they were painted on rough oblongs of plywood.

"They're very good," Sheila commented, admiring a 6"x3" depiction of a tiny sailboat on a tree-lined lake.

Joe had to agreed. The artist, an elderly man, busily creating another image on what appeared to be a piece of skirting board, had captured perfectly the fading greens and browns of autumn, and the barely ruffled surface of the lake.

Sheila made up her mind and there followed some negotiation over the price before they eventually settled on fifteen euros, and the trio moved on.

"Fifteen euros for a piece of plywood," Joe complained. "That's about twelve pounds?"

"It came out of my purse, not your wallet, Joe." Sheila reproved. "And besides, I liked it. It'll go really well in the hall by the side door."

"I notice you weren't buying, Brenda."

"I prefer a nude. Male, of course. And I don't like them painted."

Arriving back at Apartmentos Ingles, they learned that the police had gone home for the day.

"If you really need to speak to Inspector Terrones, I can telephone him for you, señor, but he will be back tomorrow."

Joe agreed to leave it at that, and they took the lift up to the seventh floor.

Stepping out onto the landing a minute later, they were confronted by an angry Ian Dimmock.

"You got us into trouble, Murray."

"Did I?"

"Yes, you did. Terrones told us off for pulling Rita from the pool this morning."

Dimmock stood head and shoulders above Joe, but while he had never been capable of physical argument, Joe had never been one to back down, either.

"If you'd listened to me, you would have left her where she

was, but you're like all Brits living here, aren't you? A smartarse."

"Don't push your luck," Dimmock bristled.

"And don't you threaten me, sunshine. Did you have some other reason for wanting her out of the pool?"

"What the hell is that supposed to mean?"

"It means she may have been dropped there deliberately, and maybe there was something on her body that might point a finger at the guy who put her there. Something that needed removing as she was pulled out of the water."

Dimmock sucked in his breath and let it out with a malevolent hiss. "You're beginning to seriously annoy me. Not a wise move"

"And you're beginning to arouse my suspicions. That's even less of a wise move, because I never go away. Never."

Joe pushed past him and into the apartment, where Sheila gave him a mock round of applause.

"Well done, Joe. We're here less than twenty-four hours and you're already ruffling feathers."

"He's a big bugger, too, isn't he?" Brenda said.

"Is that supposed to persuade me?" Joe demanded. "Interesting, though, isn't it? Almost as if he was trying to warn me off."

***

Rita Shepperton was the only topic of debate when they got to Coyote's at about 8.30pm, but while Sheila and Brenda were surprised at the levity with which some of her neighbours took Rita's death, Joe was not.

After his confrontation with Dimmock, they chose to sit apart from the residents, and Joe told Sheila and Brenda, "I said she was a wrong un, didn't I? They're all secretly glad to see the back of her."

To Joe's surprise, one person did have something to say for

Rita: Paul Wiley.

"There was nothing wrong with that woman," he declared while he pulled a round of drinks for Joe. "At least she was honest."

"Not from what I've heard," Joe replied innocuously.

Wiley's reaction came as more of a shock than a surprise. He put down the glass he was filling with Campari and rounded on Joe.

"Are you that clown from Sanford? Mate of that Robson git who was here last year?"

"Yes, I am, and less of the clown. And less of the git, come to think."

"Is he here with you?"

"No, he isn't."

"Bloody good job, too. If I ever lay eyes on him again, I'll rip his head off."

Joe looked Wiley over and tried to imagine a fight between him and George. Wiley was tall, stout and muscular, but George was beefy. He decided he did not know which way it would go.

"All I can say is, he'd give you a run for your money."

"Yeah, well I'll give you some advice for you money," Wiley snapped. "Drink your drinks and then scram. Any pal of his is not welcome here."

"Why?" Joe bleated. "What have I done? Or my friends?"

"You're a mate of his. That's enough for me."

"Now listen—"

Pauline hurried in from the outside, came to the bar, and leaned on it, lowering her voice so that only her husband and Joe could hear.

"Will you two keep your voices down?" She glared at her husband. "And you knock it off, Paul. What happened last year has nothing to do with Joe or his lady friends, and I won't have you turning custom away."

"No, but I notice you're on first name terms with him."

"I'm on first name terms with half the bloody town. If you wanna take last year out on anyone, you take it out on me, not the punters. Now, let it drop." Pauline turned to Joe. "I'm sorry. He's just got it on him. You're welcome to drink here anytime."

Joe accepted her apology and returned to his companions. He was about to tell them what had happened, when Pauline tapped him on the shoulder and said, "A word?"

Joe agreed, and followed her from the exterior seating area, on the rough tarmac of the road's turning area, where Pauline lit a cigarette, and kicked her heels as she were wondering where to begin.

"Listen, Joe, I'm sorry about Paul, but if you know what went on last year between me and George, you'll understand why he's like that."

"I do and I do," Joe agreed. "A delivery driver from Newcastle once ripped me off for a couple of cases of bacon, but I don't take it out on every Geordie who calls into my place."

"Makes sense, which is more than Paul does when he gets on about it." She took a deep drag on her cigarette. "This is all that old cow's fault. Rita Shepperton."

"Let the cat out of the bag, did she?"

"I know you shouldn't speak ill of the dead, but she was one vicious old bat. When she was younger, she was a tabloid hack, you know."

"She told me she only wrote for the broadsheets," Joe protested.

"She's a professional liar, too, then. She was an investigative reporter for one of the Sundays. This is going back years, mind you. They had ways of getting information you wouldn't believe. Anyway, somehow or another, she tumbled me and your mate, George, and she turned the screws on him. Asked him for a hundred euros to keep her mouth shut."

"And George told her where to shove it. I know." Joe

chuckled. "She tried the same trick with me yesterday. Threatened to let Sheila and Brenda's husbands know about us. Bit difficult considering they're both dead."

"Yes, well, when George told her where to go, she threatened me. I wasn't daft. I knew she wouldn't stop with a hundred euros. She'd be back week after week, so I told her more or less the same thing. And then the rotten mare told Paul."

"And it hit the fan?"

"Big time. Paul's not just a mouthpiece, you know. He knows how to look after himself. I guessed George did, too, but just to be on the safe side, George kept away from here for the last few days of his holiday."

Joe looked back at the residents from Apartmentos Ingles and smiled grimly at their jollity.

"That could pose a lot of questions."

"Sorry? Come again?"

"Nothing. Just thinking out loud."

Chapter Seven

Wednesday morning dawned, the sky once again crystal clear, holding forth the promise of another glorious and hot day.

Watching the sun rise, Joe was still brooding on the incident in Coyote's the previous night, asking himself over and over whether it could have any link with Rita Shepperton's death.

Terrones arrived at ten and after barking orders at his men, he met with Joe, Sheila and Brenda on the lawns, where he took his ease in the early sun.

Joe and his companions had chosen a table away from the other residents, so that they could not be overheard. When Terrones took the chair opposite Joe, and crossed one knee over the other leg, Sheila and Brenda sat back to let the two men talk.

"So, Señor Murray, Christobel, the receptionist, she tells me you wanted to see me yesterday. There is something you wish to tell to me?"

Joe repeated the incident with the clock and its incorrect setting, and concluded by saying, "There is something else I think you should know, but I don't know how important it is. I believe Rita Shepperton was a blackmailer."

If the inspector was put out, he did not show it. He took the information in his stride, merely pursing his lips with a slight sideways tilt of the head that was not quite a shrug. "Are you saying this as a fact, señor, or is it merely a rumour?"

"Last year, a friend of mine stayed here. He's a bit of a ladies' man, and he, er, struck up with a local barmaid. A married woman. You understand what I'm saying?"

"Perfectly," Terrones replied.

"He told me that Rita Shepperton learned of their relationship and she demanded a hundred euros to stop her telling the barmaid's husband."

"And yet he did not bring this matter to the police."

"No."

"And did he hand over this money?"

"No. He's a tough nut, is George. He wouldn't be frightened off."

Terrones waited for Joe to go on. When he did not, he said, "There is more."

"Yes. Monday, the day we arrived, I was talking to Rita, and she tried the same trick with me. She demanded money to make sure Mr Riley and Mr Jump didn't learn about me coming on holiday with their wives."

"But like your friend, you are tough man, and you did not pay."

Joe laughed. "I'm nothing like George Robson. The fact is, Peter Riley and Colin Jump have both been dead this last five or six years. Sheila and Brenda are widows and I'm divorced. Rita could have taken out a full page ad in your national newspapers for all we cared."

Terrones looked to the two women for verification and they nodded. "I see. So what is it you are suggesting, Señor Murray?"

"I was thinking if Rita tried it with George, and then with me, what are the chances that she was a professional blackmailer, and if so, wouldn't that be a great motive for murder?"

"So your friend. He is here, in Torremolinos, right now?"

"I didn't mean George. He might be a ladies' man, but he's no killer. Anyway, he's back home in England. I was thinking she may have other victims."

"Ah. Now I understand, and you are right. It is a strong motive for murder. But there is a problem with this theory.

Rita Shepperton was not murdered. As I suspected, she died of natural causes."

Joe's eyebrows rose. "You're sure?"

"We are certain. The post-mortem results show that she died of acute myocardial infarction. A heart attack."

"Heart attacks can be induced, you know. Certain drugs—"

"There was no trace of any drugs in her bloodstream," Terrones interrupted. "And that is probably the very reason she had the heart attack."

Joe's brow creased. "Sorry? I'm not with you."

"Then permit me to explain." Terrones uncrossed his legs and sat forward, leaning on the table. "When I spoke to you and your two friends yesterday, Señor Murray," he gestured good-naturedly at Sheila and Brenda, "you told me that in England, you are a private detective. My sources they tell me you have assisted the British police in a number of murder investigations. This is so?"

"I'm observant," Joe said modestly. "Not much gets past me."

"Good. Then let us see what you make of this. Rita Shepperton suffered from a heart condition and was in constant danger of, er, how do you say it … congestive heart failure. To counter the threat, she was prescribed a diuretic. Twenty milligrams, one pill per day. We found a pack of such pills in her apartment, which had been prescribed three weeks ago. Now, let us make some assumptions. Let us assume that she ordered the prescription when she was down to the final week of her previous issue. Si?"

Joe nodded. "I'm with you."

"Three weeks later, you would expect her to have completed the previous course, and have started on the new pack. This is not so?"

"Logical enough," Joe agreed.

"You would therefore expect her to have taken fourteen of the twenty-eight pills she was issued, and yet, Señor Murray,

81

she has taken only nine. Now you have to remember that we found no trace of any drugs in her bloodstream. As a detective, what would you conclude from that?"

"There are a number of possibilities," Joe admitted. "She could have misplaced the pills." He could see Terrones struggling with the word 'misplaced', and promptly translated. "Lost them." When the inspector nodded, Joe went on. "Someone could have taken them from her."

"In both cases, why then did she not approach her doctor for a new prescription? Come, Señor Murray, you are avoiding the most likely conclusion. There is more. After her heart attack, she was prescribed aspirin, seventy-five milligrams. It supports the heart. We found no such pills in her apartment, and we think she may never have had the prescription filled. The simple truth is, that Rita Shepperton was not well-organised when it came to taking her pills. This has been confirmed by Señor Holgate and Señor Olivant, and do you not agree that this is the most likely situation?"

Joe smiled weakly. "That was next on my list, and yes, it seems a strong possibility."

"And there you have it. It occurs to me that this is why she had the heart attack six weeks ago, and it is why she had one yesterday, and as we all know, the chances of surviving two heart attacks so close together is not good." Terrones relaxed a little and smiled benignly on Joe. "Do not be unhappy, señor. We are not ungrateful. We are happy when the public comes to us with information, and I shall make notes of your opinions on Rita Shepperton. But at this moment, I have no evidence to suggest that anyone else was involved in her death. I do not think that the incorrect time on Señora Riley's clock makes much difference. It simply means that Señora Shepperton went for her swim one hour after we had assumed. It would still be dark and the water it would be cold. I believe the combination of the cold water and lack of medication caused the heart attack. I stand by what I said yesterday. She was laid on the lounger at the time, tried to get up and fell into the pool, but by the time she hit the water, she was no longer breathing. She was dead." The inspector leaned back again, and lowered his sunglasses. "I am told by other residents that you have been unwell recently. Like Rita Shepperton, a heart attack."

"I did not have a bloody heart attack," Joe grumbled. Worried that Terrones would not understand his irritation, he mellowed slightly and said, "But it could have been. The symptoms were right, and I'm in the right area for one. Stress. You know. Business pressures, working too hard."

"A killer. You know, señor, I have visited your country many times. I have worked with your detectives in Scotland Yard, and I know how thorough they are."

Joe was impressed. "Really? International drug smuggling? Terrorism?"

"Football hooligans," Terrones replied with a smile. "Your country, she is beautiful, but the weather … Ah. It is so bad. The last time I was there, it rained for days on end."

"Sounds about right."

"That is why you British love to come to Spain. You know, Costa del Sol, it means, coast of the sun." Terrones gestured at the sweeping coastline, the crowded beach and the open waters of the Mediterranean. "This region it is built for pleasure."

"A bit like Brenda," Joe muttered.

The woman herself scowled and Terrones frowned.

"Señor?"

"Nothing. Sorry. Go on with what you were saying."

"Tourism is our life, Señor Murray. Without the tourist, we would be still a small fishing village. We love the visitors from Great Britain, Germany, Scandinavia. Everything here is designed for your enjoyment and relaxation. And men like you, who work too hard, men who are frequently taken from this world too early by such stresses, need the Costa del Sol. Take my advice, and enjoy it. Relax. Take life a bit easy? *Si*? If you have any evidence that Rita Shepperton was murdered, I am happy to listen, but do not go looking for that evidence. Follow your doctor's orders instead and unwind."

He stood up and offered his hand. Joe shook it.

"Thank you for your concern, señor. I will leave you to get on with your holiday."

Terrones marched off, nodding to Sheila and Brenda as he passed them.

Brenda's wandering eyes looking back over the inspector's impressive, departing frame.

"So?" Sheila asked with a steely eye on Joe.

"The man's a bloody fool if he thinks Rita died of natural causes."

"But you didn't tell him that?" Brenda asked.

"No. He told me. Didn't you hear him?"

"No, Joe. I mean you didn't tell him he was bloody fool."

"Of course not."

"It seems to me that the inspector is right," Sheila said. "And you, Joe Murray, have worked yourself up into a state over nothing."

"No. He's got it wrong. They all have. If Rita's body had been examined by an English doctor, then—"

"Enough," Sheila cut him off. "Joe, that is racism, and I've know you many years, but I have never known you to be racist."

"No. I'm not, but—"

"They're doctors, Joe," Brenda cut in. "They get the same training all over the world. They know what they're doing, and in the case of pathologists, they don't miss anything. There was nothing wrong with the post-mortem on Rita."

"All right, all right." Joe chewed spit. "So she died of a wobbler. But someone brought it on. One of her marks, I'll bet."

"If these marks exist," Sheila pointed out.

"They exist. She tried it on George, she tried it on me. There'll be others."

He looked around the lawns at the other residents sat by the bar, their good humour apparently unaffected by the events around them. As Joe watched, Juan stepped out of the apartment block, into the sunshine and looked around as if seeking something to do. Joe signalled to him.

"*Si, señor*. What can Juan do for you?"

"The police have finished with Rita's apartment?"

"*Si*. They have taken away their tape."

"Good. In that case, why don't you lend me the key so I can have a look around the place?" He smiled up. "I might be interested in renting it."

"I cannot do this, señor. There are procedures."

Joe scowled. "All right, so I wanna nosy around a bit. See what I can find out. Unofficially. No one knows but me and you."

Juan gaped convincingly. "Señor Murray, I am shocked that you would offer me twenty euros so that I can give you the key to another's apartment. I would be betraying the trust my manager puts in me if I were to take your money and give you the key."

Joe tutted. "I'll go no higher than five euros."

"Did you say fifteen?"

"Ten."

Juan looked furtively around, and slipped the key to Joe. "Please make sure no one sees you going into the apartment and give back the key to me when you are finished."

Joe smiled, handed over the money and pocketed the key under the amazed and disapproving stares of his companions.

"What are you doing, Joe?" Sheila demanded as Juan walked away.

Joe got to his feet and stretched. "Playing detective. When you're investigating a murder, you start by looking at the victim. Come on."

***

Standing outside apartment 703, Rita's place, Joe glanced furtively one way and the other to ensure they weren't being watched, then slotted the card key home. He heard the lock click, pushed the door open, ushered Sheila and Brenda in, followed them, and while Brenda parted the balcony drapes a few inches to throw some natural light into the room, he locked them in.

The apartment was laid out exactly the same as theirs, with the two settees facing other and an occasional table between them. On the sideboard stood a silver-grey laptop and behind it, a selection of books hemmed in by ornamental bookends.

Sheila scanned them. "The Writers and Artists Yearbook, Willings Press guide, The Writer's Handbook, chambers Dictionary and Thesaurus, The Oxford Dictionary of Quotations. Obviously a writer."

"She was a journalist before she retired," Joe said. "She told me." Joe clapped his hands together like a market trader about to offer an unbeatable bargain. "So where are we gonna begin?"

"I'll take the laptop," Sheila said, picking the machine up.

Joe grunted. "It wouldn't be seemly for a man to go through her clothing, so do you want to do the wardrobes, Brenda, and I'll start on these cupboards in here and the kitchen."

Brenda shrugged. "Fine. What are we looking for?"

Joe mirrored the shrug, his hands held up and open. "I dunno. Something. Anything."

"Such as?"

"I just said, I don't know."

Brenda disappeared into the large bedroom, Sheila seated herself at the dining table and switched on the laptop, while Joe moved to the kitchen and threw open the overhead cupboard doors.

The pots and pans were neatly arranged and hid nothing. The same could be said of the fridge and the larder cupboard, neither of which held much in the way of foodstuffs let alone anything else. There was nothing to be found in either the crockery cupboard or cutlery drawer, other than what he would expect, and the cooker held only those item he would anticipate finding with such an appliance. Opening the cupboards beneath the sink, he found only the usual household materials and cleaners, and enough space around them to see that there was nothing unusual.

He glanced briefly up at the water heater, fixed to the wall by the fridge, and instantly dismissed it. Rita would not be stupid enough to keep anything in there, and even if she were, the only access was via a removable lid on the top, and although it would be possible to drop something in it, she would never have been able to retrieve it.

Returning to the living room, he heard Brenda banging about in the wardrobes and cupboards in the bedroom.

She reappeared as Joe got down on his knees and began rummaging in a cupboard full of jumpers.

"You know what's missing here?" he asked. "Her phone."

Sheila looked up from the computer. "It's there, Joe. On the sideboard."

Joe followed her gaze and scowled at the telephone extension. "I meant her mobile phone."

"Perhaps she didn't have one."

"She did. She used it yesterday during the barbecue. She was hassling Holgate to make sure her burger was well done."

"So that's what we're looking—" Brenda began, only to be cut off by an exclamation from Sheila.

"Well this is odd."

Still on his knees, searching through a drawer of jumpers, Joe looked up and around at her. "What's odd?"

"The computer." Sheila gestured at the screen. "There's nothing on it … well, I say there's nothing on it. The usual software is there, but there are no documents, no photographs. Nothing, other than this single document, and that has only one line written on it." She began to read aloud. "Felicity, the records you want are safe in Atlantis."

Closing the drawer, Joe stood upright, arched his back to ease the ache, and moved to the table, where he took the machine from Sheila. Brenda crowded onto the seat next to him.

He checked the document title, *Felicity*, then read the single line of text, and shut the word processing package down. Calling up the 'Recent Documents' menu, he scanned through the short list of three documents. *Felicity* was there along with *Ipmhbuf* and *cbngpse*. When he clicked on the latter two in turn, he received the same message: *The drive or network connection that the shortcut Imphbuf.doc refers to is unavailable.*

Automatically he checked the network icon in the system tray and found it connected. "Can't be a web page, then," he muttered. "If it was, I'd be able to access it."

"It's a doc file," Brenda said. "That means it's a word processed page, not a website.

Joe opened the recycle bin, and found it empty. He tried the recent document's link again, but this time right-clicked it, and selected properties, which amongst other information, came up with the message, *F:\Imph.doc*

He lifted the machine and looked around it. Putting it down again, he said, "We're looking for either a memory stick or an expansion drive that connects through one of the USB ports."

The two women exchanged amused glances.

"Go on then, Joe," Brenda invited. "You're dying to tell us, so how do you know?"

"Drive letters on computers all go way back when. I can't remember what A and B are. Floppy discs, I think. C is the machine's hard drive. D is the CD drive when one's fitted, and this machine has one." He indicated the CD drawer to the side of the machine. "Letters after D are usually USB drives. This is drive F, and there are three USB ports on the machine, so it's one of them, and the only memory facilities I can think of which plug into a USB are memory sticks and expansion drives."

"Cameras?" Sheila suggested.

"Mp3 players," Brenda echoed.

"Camcorders?"

"You can even run your TV through the computer."

"All right, all right, but they wouldn't be identified as storage drives, would they? I repeat this is either a memory stick or an expansion drive."

Brenda looked up at the line of books on the shelves. "It couldn't be a CD?"

"Unlikely. Why?"

Brenda crossed to the bookshelves. "She said it's safe in Atlantis." She began to study the titles, cocking her head to one side to read them. "You could hide a CD in the pages of a book … if she has a book on Atlantis."

"Possible, I suppose," Joe agreed, "but unlikely. She'd need to plug a CD player into the USB port, and why bother when she has an inbuilt player?" He tapped the CD drawer of the machine. "Look for it if you want, but my guess is we're looking for a memory stick. It's easier to hide than an expansion drive."

Brenda came away from the bookshelf. "Nothing about Atlantis there anyway. Like Sheila said, they're all writers' books."

Joe pushed the machine away from him, and sat back, drumming his fingers on the table. "It's at times like this I need a smoke. It helps me think."

"Now, Joe," Sheila chided, "you're doing very well. A week without a cigarette. Don't give in."

"Yes, but I'm still going mad for one."

"Stay with the plan, Joe," Brenda urged. "Take your mind off cigarettes and tell us what she means by Atlantis?"

"Well it's an island, isn't it?"

"A continent, so they claim," Sheila said. "Its existence has never been proven, but it supposedly sat between Africa and the Americas and it sank thousands of years ago."

"So we can rule that out," Joe declared. "The chances of Rita discovering the lost continent of Atlantis and keeping it to herself are lower than a snake's doodah. That is not what she meant."

"All right, then, maestro. What else?" Brenda strummed her lips. "Is there a bar or a shop nearby call Atlantis?"

"Pass."

"Pass."

"A ship in the harbour?" Brenda suggested.

"Rita would have to know the captain or members of the crew," Joe pointed out. "Otherwise she wouldn't consider it safe." He frowned. "I think we're barking up the wrong tree here. This word Atlantis means something, and I don't think it's out there." He waved vaguely at the balcony.

"Why, Joe?"

"This Felicity, she's probably Rita's daughter or niece, or something, and Rita wanted her to have these records. They must be pretty heavy stuff, too, or why go to all the trouble of hiding them like this?"

"It may be her investment portfolio," Brenda pointed out.

"It may be," Joe agreed, "but I don't think so. You'd leave that with a lawyer or a bank, wouldn't you?"

"Could it be an anagram?" Sheila asked.

The other two exchanged semi-humorous glances.

"Why should it be, Sheila?"

"Rita did crosswords. Cryptic crosswords. Not the easy ones like you do, Joe. Those in the *Daily Express* or the *Sun*. Rita took on the really tough puzzles in *The Times* or *The Telegraph*."

Joe grimaced. "The *Daily Express* cryptic is not easy."

"Let's not get sidetracked," Brenda said. "What can we make out of Atlantis?" She dug into her bag and came out with a pen and a small diary.

Prompted by her, Joe and Sheila each took a sheet of paper from Rita's telephone pad, and all three began to write.

"I can get nails tat," Brenda said.

"I tan last," Sheila reported.

"Ants tail," Joe said.

"Sail tant,"

"Tat slain."

"Nasal tit."

"Tin atlas."

"A salt tin."

"Tan tails …" Joe trailed off. "Hang on. Did you say a salt tin, Sheila?"

She nodded and checked her work. "Yes. It's there."

All three turned their heads slowly to look at the kitchen. With a scraping of chairs on the floor tiles, they hurried for it. Brenda got there first, rooting through the cupboards and drawers, slamming them shut when she had eliminated them.

Leaning to face them through the open hatch, she held up a packet of Saxo table salt.

"No tin but there is this."

"Anything in it?" Joe demanded.

Brenda shook the packet, then flipped open the lid. "Yes. Salt."

Disappointed they returned to the table.

"Maybe it's not an anagram after all," Sheila said.

"The cryptic thing was your idea," Joe pointed out, and searched through his pockets. "Damn. I need a cigarette."

"No you don't. And I still think it may be cryptic, Joe. Not all cryptic clues are anagrams."

As Brenda rejoined them, he sat back. "All right. What else?"

"Well think about Atlantis. What's special about it?"

"It's an island," Brenda said.

"It sank," Joe replied, "but then, so did the Bismarck and the Titanic. And if she's hidden it on an island, sunken or otherwise, we could be at this for years. The thing with cryptic clues, Sheila, is they have to mean something to everyone in general or they can't be solved."

"This one doesn't," Sheila pointed out. "This is aimed specifically at Felicity, whoever she is. It doesn't have to mean anything to anyone but her."

Joe threw his hands in the air and let them fall back into his lap. "In that case, we'll never find it."

"It's under water," Brenda said so suddenly that the other two were compelled to stare.

"Brenda, I just said—"

"I heard what you said," she interrupted. "Old Holgate is the one who's deaf, not me. All I'm saying is if it were a general clue, Atlantis is under water."

The other two exchanged further glances.

"The swimming pool?" Sheila asked. "Perhaps she was in the process of hiding it when she had the heart attack. It might explain why she was out there at that hour."

"And how did she see where she was leaving it?" Joe asked. "It was pitch dark. She wouldn't be able to see and she had no torch. Besides, if this is what I think it is, you couldn't hide it under water. It would be ruined."

"You could if it were well wrapped up," Brenda said. "You hear tales of people hiding drugs and guns and things in the lavatory cistern, but they have to be well wrapped to keep them dry. At least two or three polythene bags, and tightly sealed."

Joe kicked back his chair. "Okay. Let's take a look in the khasi."

He led the way into the bathroom where he removed the lid from the lavatory cistern and peered in.

Constructed of plastic parts, there was little sign of corrosion, but the whole of the innards were covered in grime. Sheila wrinkled her nose and Joe scowled.

"Nothing," he said.

"What about the hot water?" Sheila asked.

"In the kitchen," Brenda replied and this time she led the way.

Even though he had already dismissed the idea, and now

protested about it to his companions, Joe nevertheless checked that the storage heater was switched off, and then stretched and struggled to reach the lid.

"She would have stood on a chair," Sheila said.

"I can't see her going to all this trouble," Joe grumbled while Brenda brought a chair from the living room.

"If it's as damning as you think, Joe, she will have done."

With the two women holding the chair steady, Joe climbed up, stood gingerly upright, and lifted the top off the cylinder. Peering in, he could see nothing, other than the heater element at the very bottom. He reached into it and ran his hand around the interior.

"Nothing," he complained. "Sod all."

Replacing the lid, he climbed down, Brenda took away the chair, and Joe ran the water at the sink. Pouring a little washing up liquid onto his hands, he washed them vigorously.

"We're wasting our time here," he grumbled. "We need to think about who she could have been blackmailing and why, and confront them."

"And without a shred of evidence, they'll laugh in your face," Brenda called from the front room.

"You haven't seen me cross-examine," he warned her.

Picking up a towel, drying his hands, he leaned over the sink to shut off the faucet with his elbow. As he did so, he watched the water hitting the stainless steel sink, splashing and swirling and draining through the waste.

"Underwater," he muttered.

Sheila stirred at his words. "Sorry, Joe? I was miles away. Did you say something?"

"Just thinking." He shut off the tap, threw the towel on top of the cooker, and opened the cupboard doors beneath the sink. "Underwater, you said. Suppose it's under … water?"

"Yes, Joe, but I meant—"

"I know what you meant," he interrupted, "but how cryptic is cryptic?"

Inside the cupboard was a bucket, some cleaning materials and a packet of soap powder. Joe dragged them out, got down on his knees, rolled onto his back, and shuffled under the sink, staring up.

The cupboard stank of cloying damp and bleach. He shuddered at the sight of several dead insects, trapped in old spider webs. He shuddered further at the grease and verdigris covering the pipes and underside of the bowl. But tucked into the tight gap between the unit carcase and the downward bulge of the bowl he could see something small secured to the unit by adhesive tape.

"I've found something."

"What? What is it, Joe?"

"Not sure. Gimme a minute."

He reached up and picked at it with a finger nail. Bits of damp MDF and grime came off, showering into his eye, hair and mouth. He spat them out to one side and tried again, only to pick off more muck from above.

The discomfort of his position, the awkward angle of his arm, reaching up and twisting into the narrow space, where he had little room to manoeuvre, began to tell on him.

"I can't shift it. Pass me a knife, will you?"

He relaxed a moment, easing the strain on his neck and shoulder muscles, and listened to one of this companions (he assumed Sheila) rattling through the cutlery drawer. A sharp steak knife was pressed into his hand. He reached up again and attacked the tape with it. It was easier with the knife, but it caused more filth to drop from the underside of the sink, including a decayed spider's web, which landed across his cheek.

Spitting it away, muttering soft curses, he dug at the adhesive tape.

"Must be three layers of Sellotape on this thing."

Slowly it began to peel away from the unit. Once he had enough of it free, he discarded the knife, cramped his hand and reached into the gap, gripping the loosened tape between thumb and forefinger, it took two attempts, but he finally tore it off.

Wriggling out of the cupboard, his face covered in grime, he grinned and held up a memory stick.

"Surprising what you find under other peoples' sinks, innit?"

***

Coming out of the bathroom, showered and changed into fresh shorts and an open necked, short-sleeved shirt, Joe dropped his laundry into a carrier bag, and passed through the living room to join his companions on the balcony.

Conscious of the length of time they had been in Rita's apartment, they had elected not to check the memory stick on her laptop, and instead sneaked out. Sheila had surreptitiously returned the key to Juan while Brenda went to the supermarket and Joe returned to their apartment to shower off. Still in the shower, he heard them pottering in the living room, preparing tea and putting out the cakes Brenda had bought from the shop. Brenda disturbed him only once to ask where his netbook was.

Now as he stepped from the interior to the bright, afternoon sunshine, luxuriating in the warmth, he found Sheila, a cup of tea at her elbow, poring over the netbook screen.

Careful not to trip over the mains cable which ran from the machine to an extension board, and back into the apartment, he sat between the two women, and lowered his sunglasses against the powerful ultraviolet.

Stirring sugar into his tea, helping himself to a slice of Battenberg cake, he asked, "Well?"

"I don't think you're going to like this, Joe," Sheila replied, raising her reading glasses and pushing the machine to him. "I believe you got it right when you said this machine contains important information, because every file is locked with a password."

Swallowing a piece of cake, swashing it down with a swallow of tea, Joe stared glumly at the files. There were only a dozen, all Microsoft Word documents, but as Sheila promised when he tried to open one, a message box appeared demanding the password.

He typed in 'atlantis' and it rejected it. He tried 'Shepperton' and was once more rejected. He began to fool around with more obvious words like Apartmentos Ingles, Torremolinos, Rita, even Felicity, but it got him nowhere.

He chewed and swallowed the last of his Battenberg. "Know what I think? I think the crackpot document titles are in some kind of code, and I think the password to the files is the solution to that code."

Sheila turned the computer to herself. "Why do you say that, Joe?"

"Because the doc names make no sense. What the hell does imphbuf mean? It has to be a code."

"Or an acronym," Brenda suggested. "In my purple, er, headdress, er, be upstanding, fool."

"We don't know that she owned a purple headdress, dear," Sheila responded.

"If she did I never saw it," Joe commented.

"I'm not saying that's what it stands for. I was giving it as an example."

"That's one hell of a long password," Joe reflected. "So what can you get from L-F-F-M-J-H-B-O."

Brenda took the computer and studied it. "Look for father Michael's joyous, holy, brotherly order." She grinned at their astonished stares.

"Is the sun getting to you, Brenda?" Joe demanded.

"Well, it's making me feel frisky."

"That's not what—"

"I'll tell you what I think," Brenda interrupted. "I think we should put the damned computer away, and get out for a walk along the seafront. It'll do us all the power of good."

Sheila gulped down her tea. "And I think you're dead right, Brenda."

Chapter Eight

"Señor Murray"

At the sound of Juan's voice, Joe stirred and opened his eyes. "Hmm. What?"

The janitor appeared worried. "I am not sure how to tell you this."

Thursday morning had dawned hot, the sky clear once more, and Joe, by now quite accustomed to take his ease in the sunshine, had managed to put aside the problems of Rita Shepperton and her secret documents. They had enjoyed an excellent meal at the Bullhorn restaurant, and for a change of both scene and company, they visited O'Malley's, an Irish bar further down the street from Apartmentos Ingles, putting some distance between them and the residents of Little England.

Sleeping off the late night and early-ish morning, with Sheila and Brenda alongside him by the pool, Joe was in no mood to deal with Juan angling for more money. He raised his sunglasses and screwed up his eyes to counter the fierce ultraviolet. "Try telling it straight, son. It usually works for me."

Juan coughed as if trying to hide embarrassment. "One of the maids, Sarita, she has been into Rita Shepperton's room and the place has been, er, trashed."

Joe sat upright, Brenda and Sheila honed their attention on the conversation.

Joe controlled his racing thoughts. "The first question is what was this Sarita doing in there?"

Juan shrugged. "I can only say, Mr Murray, that she is an

honest woman. I think it was genuine mistake. The maids, they come in only twice a week."

"I'll buy that," Joe agreed, "but even so, she should have been told that Mrs Shepperton was dead and no one was supposed to go in there."

"I tell her this," Juan replied, "but she did not listen to me. I do not think, señor, that she is thinking to steal anything. It is not Sarita to steal."

"Let's put that aside, Joe," Sheila suggested. "Juan, did you say the room had been ransacked?"

Juan frowned. "Ransacked?"

"Trashed," Joe translated.

"*Si, señor.*"

"Has anything been taken?" Brenda wanted to know.

The janitor shrugged. "I do not know, señora. Everything is everywhere. It is impossible for me to know."

Joe struggled to his feet and patted his pockets. "You stop me from smoking just when I need a cigarette the most."

"It's for your own good, Joe," Brenda said, leaving her lounger. "Let's take a look at Rita's place, just to take your mind off tobacco."

Joe nodded to Juan. "Lead on."

"Que?"

"Rita's apartment. Let's take a look."

With Sheila and Brenda bringing up the rear, Joe followed Juan around the corner of the building, where the shade offered some respite from the heat, and in through the main entrance.

Once on the first floor landing, Juan unlocked and opened the door and Joe stepped cautiously in, as if expecting someone to leap out and attack him.

There was no need for caution. Whoever had been in the place was no longer there, but they had certainly left their calling card.

As Juan had promised, Rita's effects were spread everywhere.

The drawers had been pulled out and emptied on the floor. The overhead kitchen cupboards were left wide open, many of the pots and pans removed. Even the fridge and freezer door were left open.

Joe bent to check beneath the sink where he had found the memory stick the previous day, but learned that none of the utensils or packages had been moved.

"They were looking for the memory stick or Rita's files," he said to his companions. "It's the only place that hasn't been disturbed because they thought they could see everything just by opening the cupboard doors." He looked around the remainder of the room. "At a guess, I'd say nothing has been taken."

"Wrong, Joe," Sheila said from the living room. "The laptop is missing."

"Damn." Joe spat the word out. "Juan, who else would have a key to this apartment?"

"I do not know, señor. No one should have one but Señora Shepperton and us."

"And yet the door hasn't been forced," Joe muttered. "Which means that someone else does have a key. Who?" he stroked his chin thoughtfully.

"It has to be one of the residents on this landing, Joe," Brenda told him. "They were the only people she had anything to do with, and she didn't trust the Span … you and your people, Juan."

"I know this," Juan said.

"In that case …" Joe turned a broad smile on the janitor. "Juan, do you have to report this to the police?"

"I should do, señor."

"Well, whoever it was, they haven't broken in, have they? I mean, the door wasn't forced."

"No, señor."

"So if we kept quiet about it for a few days, we could appear to be no wiser, couldn't we?"

Juan frowned again. "I am sorry, señor, I don't understand what you are trying to do."

"Look, if we don't say anything about Sarita going into the room, then it will be like no one knows what has happened, won't it? Sarita won't get into trouble, and no one will know what's happened except the person or persons who did it."

Juan did not appear to be any the wiser, so Joe turned to his companions. "You explain it."

"I don't think I can, Joe," Sheila said, "because I don't understand what it is you're trying to do."

Joe huffed out his breath. "Lord preserve me from stupid women and ESOL candidates." He stared at Sheila as if by doing so he could mentally transmit his thoughts. "Let me spell it out. Someone has been in here. What were they looking for?"

"Valuables," Brenda said brightly.

"*Sí*," Juan agreed. "Or drugs. Drugs are easy to sell to the young people on holiday."

"All right, I agree," Joe said. "But suppose they weren't. We're agreed that they had a key, aren't we. How many burglars would you find with a key to this room? Not many, I'll bet. So we're all agreed that they were looking for the files I found?"

"With you so far," Brenda said.

"Who's the likeliest candidate?"

"Haven't a clue," Brenda volunteered.

"Me neither," Sheila concurred.

"And I do not understand what you are talking about. You found a file here? It could have belonged to the plumber who comes in the winter to—"

"It's not that kind of file, Juan. I mean a file full of information." Joe dug into his shirt pocket and drew out the memory stick. "Computer files."

"Ah. Now I understand. You think it is one of the people Rita was blackmailing?"

All three stared. "Blackmailing?" Sheila asked. "So you

know?"

Juan nodded. "Si, but it is not, how do you say, plain knowledge—"

"Common knowledge?" Joe suggested with raised eyebrows.

"Si. Common knowledge. But I hear things when I am working round the building, and I believe Rita Shepperton was blackmailing some of her neighbours."

The three exchanged glances again.

"So you were right all along, Joe, and it explains why the documents are password protected," Brenda said.

Joe sneered. "As if we didn't know that too."

"We need to crack those codes. I have to apologise, Joe. Your reading of the situation was spot on." Sheila half turned to Juan. "Do you know which of her neighbours she was supposed to be blackmailing?"

He shrugged. "I know only what I hear as I do my work. There is the colonel. He complained he could not afford it much longer. At first, I think he is paying for that which Juan can get for nothing. *Entiende*?" He augmented the question with a smile and leer at Brenda's cleavage.

"I think we get the picture," Joe said. "Go on."

"But then I hear Rita say, he will pay and do as he is ordered or there will be bigger price and I think she is threatening to expose him for something."

"But you don't know what?"

"No, señor. But he is not the only one. I see señor Keeligan go for prescriptions every month, and I wonder why he is so sly about it. Why does he not want Mrs Keeligan to know, and why does he go for Rita Shepperton when she can go herself? Señor Olivant, too, he supplies her with food and drink, and all the time I am wondering what does she know about these people that they would do this?"

"And you never mentioned it to anyone?" Sheila asked.

"No, señora. I speak to my boss, of course, but only, er … gossip. You know. She tells me it is none of my affairs and to

102

get on with my work." He shrugged. "So I get on with my work."

Joe dug into his pocket and came out with a five euro note. "You kept quiet about that, Juan, so you can keep quiet about this, too, just for the next few days." He handed over the money. "Okay?"

Juan grinned. "My lips are peeled, señor."

"He means sealed," Brenda said, leading the way out.

"We guessed," Joe replied.

Stepping back out on the access deck, Sheila and Brenda turned right, towards the exit, but Joe turned left.

"You go on," he said. "I'm gonna work on that code."

"Joe, you're supposed to be taking it easy."

"Boredom is just as stressful as overworking," he told them. "I'll be in the apartment. Gimme a shout when it's time to eat."

***

With the time passing one in the afternoon, and the hottest part of the day approaching, Sheila and Brenda returned to the apartment to find Joe brainstorming the codes. The floor was littered with screwed up and torn sheets of notepaper, most of it covered with his untidy scrawl.

Sheila nudged Brenda and indicated a slight haze of smoke in the room, picked out by the strong sunlight coming from the balcony.

"I'll have him for that," Brenda promised in a low whisper.

"No," Sheila urged, and nodded back through the door. To Joe she said, "Won't be a minute, dear."

They returned to the landing, closing the door behind them.

"He is smoking," Brenda grumbled.

"Yes. He is. But it's not much otherwise the room would stink of it. Brenda, let's be sensible. He's smoked for years and we demanded that he stop just like that." Sheila snapped her fingers. "It's hard. I know. Peter never stopped, you know. He

103

tried, but it was too damned difficult."

"Yes but—"

"We know Joe has cut back to almost nothing," Sheila said, cutting in on her friend. "He's done really well, and we can encourage him to take the final step from a reduced intake. Let's just be glad he's cut back as far as he has done. We'll sort him out when we get home."

Brenda appeared doubtful. "Well, if you're sure …"

"Let's play his game for a time." Sheila led the way back in. "Sorry about that."

Brenda beamed on him. "How are you doing, Master Spy? Cracked the Russian secrets and staved off the end of civilisation as we know it, yet?"

Sheila laughed. "Have you not solved it yet, Joe? Perhaps it's a secret recipe, so think in terms of meat pies."

In exasperation, Joe tore another sheet from his notebook, screwed it up and threw it across the room, missing the waste bin by several feet. "You have a go," he grumbled. "I can't make head nor tail of any of them."

"That's no reason to litter the floor," Brenda said, picking up the latest addition to the waste. Carrying the bin, she began to go round the room collecting crumpled sheets.

Sheila stared at the netbook screen. "Oh, well, now that we know who we think the passwords refer to, the code is simple."

"No it isn't," Joe protested. "I've been here three bloody hours trying to—"

"Like all codes, it's a substitution." Sheila pointed to the word Lffmjhbo on the screen. "Let's assume that this is one of the names that Juan gave to us. Now who do we know who has an eight-letter surname, with a double letter immediately after the initial?"

Joe shrugged. "Sylvia Goodson."

"Quite. But Sylvia isn't here, and anyway, her name has only seven letters. I was thinking more of the people in residence. As I said, one of the names Juan gave to us, and right away that makes me think of Keeligan."

Joe looked blankly at it. "The right number of letters, but where do you get Keeligan from?"

"I just told you. A name with eight letters, with a double letter following the initial. Keeligan is the only one I can think of amongst the residents." Sheila studied for a few more moment and her face lit. "Oh. Of course. Each letter of the alphabet has been moved one place. B stands for A, C stands for B and so on.

With a frown, Joe wrote it out in capital letters on his notebook, then followed Sheila's advice.

L-F-F-M-J-H-B-O

K-E-E-L-I-G-A-N

"My God, you're right."

"Of course, I'm right. Why not try it as the password?"

Joe called up the document Lffmjhbo and when prompted for the password, typed in Keeligan. The machine threw it out again.

"Nope. No—"

"You used a capital 'K'," Sheila pointed out. "Try it all in lowercase."

Joe did so, and to his delight the file burst to life, filling the screen.

"We're in." Leaning forward, he read the screen, and his face fell. It was more of the same gobbledygook. "She's only gone and encoded the whole document."

Sheila drew up a chair. "Looks like we've got a busy afternoon then, doesn't it? If we work together, we'll soon know everything that Rita Shepperton did …"

It was a long, painstaking and arduous task. First Joe had to translate the passwords, then open the files before they could begin on the encrypted documents.

"It must have taken her ages to do this," Brenda observed. "You know. Write out the files then transcribe all the letters."

Joe gestured at their balcony where the sun blazed. "What

else was she gonna do with her time on the Costa del Sol?"

Time passed. Brenda made tea, Sheila made sandwiches, Joe set the table and they worked through lunch, each tackling particular sentences. Outside, holidaymakers played on the beach, the illegal traders plied their wares or ran on warning of the *Policia Local approaching*. Crowds ebbed and flowed through bars and restaurants. Joe made tea, Sheila dug out the cakes and Brenda set the table out on the balcony, and they worked through an afternoon snack, the netbook burning away in front of them, with the complex codes permanently on screen.

By five o'clock it was done, and Joe gathered the notes together to read through them with the satisfaction of a job well done.

The confusing sentence, *uipnbt ipmhbue boe ujn dpmmjot tupmf uxp ivoesfe boe gjguz uipvtboe qpvoet pg uifs dmjfout npofz* now made perfect sense as *Thomas Holgate and Tim Collins stole one hundred thousand pounds of their clients' money*, and they had translated *ibo ejnnpdl jt ibwjoh bo bggbjs xjui boo cbngpse* to the more informative *Ian Dimmock is having an affair with Ann Bamford*.

In addition to the revelations on Holgate, Dimmock and Ann Bamford, there was also a reference to the Olivants as having left England along with the church restoration fund amounting to some £30,000, and Maurice Keeligan involved in an affair with Pauline Wiley, about which Pauline's husband, whom Joe knew to be short-tempered, knew nothing, and further references to the pasts of Ann Bamford and the Acres. Finally, he found an admission by Rita that when she first arrived at Apartmentos Ingles, she and Holgate had been involved in an affair.

"Rather him than me," Joe said, keeping his voice low to avoid the risk of being overheard on the balconies either side. "This information is pure dynamite."

"And it may put a different picture on Rita's death," Sheila said, keeping her voice to a conspiratorial whisper. "It also clears up the alleged burglary. Someone really was looking for this memory stick."

"We really should take it to Terrones," Joe said with a yawn. Reaching to the netbook, he switched it off. "But to be fair, we need to know what the … er … accused make of it all. It can wait until tomorrow and I'll have a word with them. For now, I need a nap and then I have to get on the web."

"Whatever for, Joe?" Brenda asked.

"I need to follow up the tale of Holgate and the Olivants, the Acres and Ann Bamford. If there is any truth in either of them, they'd have been reported in the media back home."

"It would be years ago, Joe," Sheila objected.

"The internet never forgets." He picked up the netbook and smiled broadly at them. "You did well, both of you. Dinner's on me tonight. What do you fancy? Egg and chips?"

Brenda sidled up to him. "If you're looking for a wild night, Joe, I'm with you, but I'll need a lot more than egg and chips to stoke up my energy levels."

Sheila giggled. "Leave him alone, Brenda. You don't want to give him another heart attack."

"If I did, the undertaker would never get the smile off his face."

***

The interior of the restaurant was dimly lit by candles, but on the pavement outside, they were able to take advantage of the early evening sun as it dipped towards the horizon.

Joe had opted for a well done steak, Sheila nibbled at a vegetarian quiche, while Brenda tackled a half chicken with gusto. And while they ate, Joe brought them up to date with his researches.

"There are half a dozen files on that memory stick and I can't get into them. Your password idea doesn't work with them, Sheila. The rest of it checks out. Holgate was involved in some shady property deal, the Olivants disappeared with the restoration fund and the Acres threw their daughter out because she was involved in some drug scene. She was found dead a few days later. Nothing suspicious about the death, but the Acres got some really bad press. Ann Bamford has a past she'd rather other people didn't know about, and Dimmock is playing away from home."

"So Rita's reports were accurate?" Sheila asked.

Joe sliced through a piece of steak. Chewing on it, he swallowed, washed it down with a sip of red wine, and nodded. "By and large, yes. The Acres haven't done anything illegal, but they came out here to avoid the hammering they took in the tabloids. The Olivants and Holgate are a different pan of chips. I need to speak to them but they could be hauled back home and into court for what they did."

Brenda, her knife and fork laid on the plate while she held the chicken and chewed on it, whipped grease from her chin. "What about the other tales? Dimmock, Ann Bamford and Maurice Keeligan?"

"Well, obviously, those kind of tales don't make the papers, but Rita got it right about Ann Bamford. She was prosecuted for soliciting so many times that she eventually got a three-month stretch for it. I'm guessing Rita was right about Keeligan and Dimmock, too. She hit the mark on everyone else."

"How much was she taking from them?" Sheila asked.

"She doesn't say." Joe grinned and speared a couple of chips with his fork. "But I'll find out."

Brenda dropped the chicken back on the plate, and burped softly. "Excuse me. That was excellent. All I need now is another flagon of ale." She swallowed a mouthful of wine. "Tell you what's interesting. How come so many, er, iffy people came together in the one apartment block? And all on the same floor."

Sheila pushed her plate away and sat back, replete, basking in the sunshine. "I think that is an excellent question, Brenda. Joe?"

He chewed through the last of his steak, dropped the knife and fork, and emptied his glass. Dabbing his lips with a black napkin, he said, "Rita doesn't comment on that, but she does make one interesting observation. Quote: Colonel Holgate knows so many people: unquote. He sold property in England years ago, didn't he? What price he found these people, the Olivants and Acres, not necessarily by accident, and invited them to rent at Apartmentos Ingles."

"Why would he do that?" Brenda asked.

"I don't know, but I can guess. He has something to do with the building. I just said, he sold property for a living. Could it be that Apartmentos Ingles was in his portfolio? All right, so the apartments are rented, but he'll still get a dip on the rental income, won't he?" Dragging the ashtray to him, he dipped into his pockets and came away frustrated again. "God, I need a smoke."

"No you don't," Sheila assured him. "So you're suggesting that Holgate actually sought these people out."

Joe nodded. "He still reads the Brit newspapers, doesn't he? They all do. Let's imagine that ten years ago he reads of the Olivants legging it with the church funds. Let's also imagine that later on he goes looking for them. And when they meet, he puts the proposition to them. 'I'm in the same boat as you two, but I have this little place in Torremolinos where I can hide away. Fancy joining me?' Holgate has been here a lot longer than any of the others. He knows a lot of faces in this part of the world. Later, he reads of the Acres and their attempt to escape the paparazzi. He goes in search of them and finds them."

"And Rita, and the Keeligans, Dimmock, Bamford?"

"Dunno about them," Joe admitted, "but probably something similar, except that these people are not on the run.

109

They're just looking for somewhere to rent. All right, so they're having it off with each other, but hell, that's common enough with people in these places, isn't it?"

Brenda guffawed loudly. "Common enough in Sanford, never mind Torremolinos."

Her laughter attracted the attention of the waiter and Joe spent a moment explaining that they needed nothing other than the bill.

"So what are you going to do, Joe?"

"What I always do," he said, digging out his wallet. "Ask questions." He took out his credit card. "Remember what I've always told you. Most people are voice operated, and all you have to do is ask the right questions. I still have some research to do, but I'll be ready for them by tomorrow."

The waiter returned with their bill. Joe dealt with it, and dug into his pocket for five euros, which he left on the table as they prepared to leave.

"Where next? Coyote's?"

"Considering Pauline is named and shamed in the documents, it sounds like a good place to start," Brenda said.

They stepped out of the restaurant, onto the pavement, and ambled along the seafront towards Apartmentos Ingles.

"I think Holgate dropped a brick when he dragged Rita Shepperton into the place," Joe said. "He had a nice little number going. The apartments all rented out, making him a bob or two, and then she come along; a former dirt-digger for the tabloids back home. Not only was she able to dig the dirt, but she was happy to turn the screws on them."

"And he's your prime suspect?" Brenda asked. "Despite the fact that Terrones has told you she died of a heart attack."

The sun stood just above the horizon, its colour changed to a glorious scarlet, the long shadows highlighting the deepened creases in Joe's brow. Along the promenade, other people paused to watch the spectacle.

"It's a problem," Joe admitted, "but like I said to Terrones, there are ways of bringing on a heart attack. Pushing her into a cold swimming pool in the dark may well have been enough."

"What did Terrones tell you?" Sheila scolded. "If it had happened that way, she would still have been breathing when she went into the pool, and there would be water in her lungs. There wasn't. She was dead before she went into the water, Joe."

His craggy features looked all the more rugged in the dying embers of the sunset, taking on a distant, contemplative quality. "It's all coincidence is what you're telling me, and I don't accept that. She has all this dirt on them and then she conveniently dies in the swimming pool." He sat on the low wall, watching the sun, now a half ball resting on the sea. "The big problem, Sheila, is not that they found water in her lungs but that they *didn't* find water in her lungs."

Sheila sat one side of him, Brenda the other.

"What do you mean?" Brenda asked.

The sun appeared to be moving faster now, sinking quickly under the water.

"Terrones says she'd been for a swim. She got out, climbed onto the lounger, then the heart attack hit her. Death by heart attack isn't instantaneous, is it? She may have been struggling for breath, certainly, but she hadn't stopped breathing. How could she? If, as he suggests, she stood up, she must have been breathing. Are we really expected to believe that she fell and rolled into the pool and stopped breathing all in those few seconds?"

A final bead of crimson disappeared beneath the horizon and Joe stood up. All around them, others picked up their evening walk along the seafront.

"She died somewhere else, and the splash you heard, Sheila, was not the sound of her falling into the pool, but someone else dropping her in."

Chapter Nine

Stepping out of the bottom gate onto the promenade, Joe took a drag and blew smoke out into the fresh, morning air. He glanced worriedly over his shoulder and up at the seventh floor, worried for a moment that one or both of his companions may have spotted the smoke.

"Sod it," he muttered. "Whose life is it, anyway?"

He recalled Rita telling him that Holgate took coffee at Chico's every day around ten in the morning. Walking along the seafront, ignoring the Moroccan and Tunisian traders hawking their fake goods, savouring the light ozone carried on a light breeze, he found the colonel right where Rita had said he would be.

Greeting Holgate with a smile, Joe said, "I've been looking for you. Mind if I join you?"

Holgate lowered his newspaper and smiled wanly. "Not at all, old man. Glad of the company." He raised a hand and snapped his fingers at the waiter. *"Café con leche. Dos. Pronto."*

Joe frowned and Holgate narrowed dismissive eyes on him.

"You don't approve?"

"Damn right, I don't," Joe replied. "I run a trucker's café in West Yorkshire—"

"So you said." There was no mistaking the snobbish disdain in the older man's interruption.

"I'm told I'm grumpy, snappy and rude with my customers. Maybe, maybe not. I don't have time to stop and worry about it. And they give me some stick back, but if anyone spoke to me or my staff the way you just spoke to the waiter, I'd throw them out."

"Have to do it, Murray. Your typical Spaniard is lazy and surly. They need a kick up the backside, make 'em work. Show 'em who's boss."

Joe shook his head. "And people wonder why we Brits have such a bad reputation abroad."

Holgate put his newspaper to one side and sneered. "Don't tell me you're one of these modern, politically correct types. Let me tell you something, Murray, it's exactly that kind of attitude that lost us the empire, and our place in the world."

"Funny," Joe replied as the waiter approached with their coffee, "because I'd say it was your attitude that brought about the British decline. Overwhelming arrogance with no substance."

The waiter delivered the coffee. Joe nodded. "*Gracias.*"

"No problem, señor." The waiter placed the bill at Holgate's elbow and without looking at the colonel, wandered off.

"See," Joe said. "One kick up the arse from you, and you have open warfare, one word of thanks from me and we have what the French call *entente cordiale.*"

"You've made your point, Murray. Don't expect me to agree."

"I don't. But tell me, Holgate, does your narrow-minded vision of this world include the internet? Or did Dimmock have it right when he said you didn't understand it?"

The colonel harrumphed. "Quite what it has to do with Dimmock, I don't know but he's right. I know nothing about it. Never needed it in my day." He picked up his newspaper and dropped it again. "This was enough. This and a telephone for field communications."

"Shame," Joe said. "I'm in my fifties and I make an effort to keep up with technology. You're less than ten years older than me and you're still living in the Stone Age … Not at all like your friend Rita."

Holgate sipped his coffee and sighed. "Is there some point

113

to this? I come here to study the markets over a cup of coffee every morning. I don't object to a little friendly conversation, but it seems to me, you're going out of your way to look for an argument."

Joe cracked a sachet of sugar, poured it into his coffee and stirred. "I'm getting there." He picked up the cup and sipped approvingly. "Ah. Excellent. Can't drink coffee in Holland, you know, but I find it quite acceptable in Southern Europe." He put the cup down. "You're, how old again? Sixty-three?"

"What of it?"

"And you've been living here since the mid eighties?"

"Did I tell you this the other day?"

"I think Rita did, to be honest. I'm never much good with numbers unless they have a pound sign in front of them, and I'm on some strong painkillers, which made the old brain a bit sluggish, but when I worked it out, I figured you were thirty-five-ish when you first moved down here."

"Thirty-seven as a matter of fact," Holgate snapped. "But again, I fail to see what business it is of yours."

Joe smiled, but there was no warmth in his words. "Bit young to have made Colonel, weren't you?"

Holgate appeared taken aback. "Well, er, exceptional, certainly. But not—"

"If you joined at aged eighteen, it would still be near impossible," Joe interrupted. "Course, you could be a *lieutenant* colonel, and I suppose you could legitimately be addressed as colonel at your time of life."

"Well, naturally, I, er—"

"And this is another area where the internet really comes into its own," Joe cut in again. "As a research tool, it's brilliant. Not perfect, but adequate for our purposes. I checked on Colonel Thomas Holgate of the High Peak Infantry. No trace of him. I also checked on Lieutenant Colonel Thomas Holgate. No trace of him, either."

Joe passed a moment to see if his words were having the

desired effect. It was difficult to tell under the leathery tan, but he guessed Holgate's colour was rising.

"Are you suggesting—"

Joe interrupted for the third time. "There are records of a *Corporal* Thomas Holgate of the High Peak Infantry. Interesting man. In the mid seventies, he spent a year in the glasshouse at Colchester for some kind of fraud, after which he was given a dishonourable discharge." Joe smiled. "There were even pictures of him from some newspaper archives. The Derby Express or something. After his release and discharge, he disappeared for a few years, and then suddenly this company, Collins and Holgate, based in Derby, turned up, selling property in Spain. They did well out of it, too, until the mid eighties when suddenly Collins disappeared with a large amount of money belonging to the company's clients. The feeling was he'd skipped it to the Costa del Sol, which back then was also known as the Costa del Crime. Britain had no extradition treaty with Spain, and it wasn't reinstated until 1985, so a lot of our major criminals hid out down here."

There was no mistaking the worry in Holgate's eyes.

"Without Collins, the cops got their claws into Holgate, who maintained he was innocent. He was released on bail, and he, too, disappeared, and once again, the cops tried to find him here. But they never did. Neither Thomas Holgate nor Tim Collins were ever seen again. The Spanish authorities had no trace of them ever landing here, but they did find a man name Tom Hollins had entered the country. Trouble was, by the time they'd learned that he came through Malaga airport, he'd disappeared. And like the other two, he's never been heard of since."

He waited for a response. Holgate picked up his cup with a trembling hand. After drinking, he dabbed at his mouth with a serviette. "I, er, I'm not sure I should say anything."

"Well you'd better," Joe retorted. "Because if you don't I'm gonna draw my own conclusions, and you won't like them.

Y'see, Holgate, I don't think Tim Collins ever existed. I think he was a figment of your imagination dreamt up so you could rip off your clients to the tune of a hundred and thirty thousand pounds."

Holgate leapt to his own defence. "You're wrong, Murray. You're jumping to the same conclusion as the police did, but Collins did exist and he was my business partner. Look, I freely admit the scams I pulled in the army and I served my time for them. When I came out of Colchester, I had nothing. Nothing at all, I went home to Derby and took the first job I could find. It was with an estate agent. I did well. If you're going to pull the wool over peoples' eyes as I did in the army, you need a glib tongue, and it's just as important in honest business. So I made progress. I met Tim Collins on a management course. He was impressed with my ability, and we got to know each other fairly well. Eventually, he came to me with a proposition. Selling Spanish property to Brits. He would put up the capital and I would handle sales. The salary and commission were like telephone numbers. So I took him at his word and I earned those telephone numbers. And I tell you now, Murray, those sales were genuine. I visited the properties, I saw them, I met with satisfied clients. Everything was above board and I was happy. By the early eighties, I was pulling down fifty thousand a year."

"So what went wrong?"

Holgate was a beaten man. His jowly features aged and his eyes lost their sparkle. Vengeful anger twisted his normally placid face into a mask of pure hatred, but when he spoke it was with the sadness of resignation.

"Tim was what went wrong. Three years down the line, he offered me a junior partnership, and I took it. Cost me most of my savings, but hell, I was suddenly making even more money. Bear in mind that all monies were held in offshore accounts. Tim advised me to do the same with the bulk of my income, and I did. I lived very frugally, and it saved me a fortune in

116

taxes and contrary to popular opinion, it is not illegal. As it turned out, I was bloody glad I did, too. Tim spent a lot of time away from the office, negotiating with developers all over Spain, and, I repeat, they were all genuine. Every single deal was honest and above board." Holgate sighed. "Then, sometime early in, oh, eighty-five, I think, he came in with a fresh deal in the Canary Islands. There was a building moratorium coming up in Los Christianos and Playa de Las Américas. We needed to move these apartments double quick. I got my sales team onto it, and we shifted over a hundred apartments in three weeks. An absolute record. Two days after the final deal was signed, Tim disappeared along with a hundred and twenty-seven thousand pounds of deposits most of which was supposed to go to the developers. A day later, the fraud squad turned up, went through the files like a dose of salts and arrested me. The development didn't even exist. It was a huge scam and Tim had successfully pulled it off. He even conned me. But the cops couldn't find any trace of him and, like you, they assumed he never existed. But he did. And the tale as you're telling it, is not accurate. I was not released on bail. I was released. Full stop. No charges were ever preferred against me. I was not guilty."

"And I suppose all those clients were happy with that, were they?"

"Were they hell as like. I was a man hounded, so I did the obvious thing. Hopped on a plane and came here, and the only thing I was guilty of at the time was using a false passport in the name of Tom Hollins."

"Why?" Joe demanded. "If you were not guilty, why run? Why use a false passport?"

"I just told you. Guilt by association," Holgate argued. "I was a partner in the business. Even though I was innocent, there were those who did not believe it, and one or two of them were, shall we say, not averse to using violence. I had to get out."

Joe considered the explanation. "You must have had a tidy amount in your offshore accounts to support you for the last twenty-five years?"

"I had a fair bit, yes, but I also invested heavily." Holgate lifted his newspaper again. "Those investments are what I live on now and they're drying up." He dropped the paper on the table again.

"All right," Joe said, "Let's say I believe you. Why are you still hiding? What are you afraid of? It's a quarter of a century, now. It'll have all blown over."

"The criminal element doesn't believe in a statute of limitations. If they find me, I am a dead man."

Joe shook his head. "So if you knew Collins was down here, why didn't you make an effort to find him? Hand him over to the mob."

"I looked for him and I found him … dead," Holgate admitted. "It took me two years to track him down, but I finally saw a newspaper report from Marbella confirming his death. Sadly, someone else got to him first. I can only assume it was one of the investors. They slit his throat."

Joe whistled. "So if they twigged you, the same thing could happen."

Holgate nodded unhappily. "I swear to you, Murray, everything I'm telling you is gospel. If I could have got to him, I'd have forced him back to Blighty and made him face up to it. Anything to take the pressure off me, but these people got there first. His murder is, technically, unsolved. How do I know the buggers aren't out there still looking for me?"

Joe finished his coffee. "So how much was Rita taking from you?"

"I don't know what you mean."

Joe scowled. "You seriously think I got all this from the internet? The files you were looking for when you broke into her apartment the night before last? You couldn't find them because I already had them. She had you banged to rights, and she was screwing you to the ground for some serious money. Now how much?"

Holgate's face ran the gamut of emotions, from shock, when Joe accused him of breaking into Rita's apartment, through fear and finally to misery. "Five hundred a month."

"Euros?"

The colonel shook his head. "Pounds sterling, if you please."

"And how long has this been going on?"

Holgate shrugged. "Seven, eight months. Perhaps a year."

"So it's already cost you anything up to six thousand. That, Holgate, is a tasty motive for murder."

The accusation stung Holgate into retaliation. "I did not kill her. For God's sake, man, if you've really seen the information she had, you must know that she and I were, er, romantically involved when she first came here. I loved her. And if someone broke into her apartment, it was not me. I'd look at Pinero if I were you." He held up both hands as a gesture of surrender. "All right, all right. I'm not sorry she's dead. A vindictive, vicious old hag. That's what she was. And if you have her files, well, I suppose the only thing I have to worry about is whether it will cost me more or whether you'll turn them over to the police. But I swear I had nothing to do with her death or with any break-in. For God's sake, man, look at me. What use would I be as a burglar at my age? I can't even hear well enough to keep lookout for someone else."

Joe picked up the bill, read €2.50 and dug into his wallet for a five euro note, then signalled the waiter who came across and took it.

"Why did you pay up?" Joe demanded. "What the hell were you worried about? That she'd pass it on to the police? She was blackmailing you, man. No way would she have gone to the cops."

"Rita Shepperton didn't threaten to tell the police. She was a journalist, remember. She was going to sell the story to the media." His eyes were haunted by the spectre of fear. "Do you think I want to end up like Tim Collins? I didn't want to spend the rest of my life looking over my shoulder." He seemed to wither and shrink into his jacket.

Joe slotted the information into his compartmentalised mind. "Right. Let's move on to other matters. You say you have investments and they pay handsomely. Apartmentos Ingles is one of them, isn't it?"

Holgate was surprised. "How on earth did you guess?"

"It wasn't a guess. It was a deduction. See, here's my problem. Rita had you nailed, but she also had others in the complex. The Olivants and the Acres, two sets of people who don't really want the British media to know where they are. Now I ask myself, how much of a coincidence is it when three sets of people, you, the Acres and the Olivants all come to be living in the same apartment block in Torremolinos. The answer is, it isn't a coincidence. You drew those couples into Apartmentos Ingles, didn't you?"

"I have to hand it to you, Murray, you've put quite a lot together over the last forty-eight hours."

"That's because I'm smarter than most Little Englanders, including you. Now tell me how you got them there."

Holgate's shoulders slumped. "It wasn't difficult. I keep abreast of events back home. I read of the Olivants and went looking for them. Found them further up the coast at Almeria. Talked frankly to them, and a month later they took the apartment next door but one to me. Not long after that, I was looking for the Acres. They were living inland. Place called Mijas, about twenty kilometres from here. Told them I understood their position and that they could live here quite economically. They came down, looked the place over, and they're now in the apartment next to door to the one you've rented."

"And you did this because they were easy blackmail targets."

"Nonsense," Holgate snapped. "I've never blackmailed anyone in my life. I did it because I needed to see these apartments rented out more than they were. I have money tied up in Apartmentos Ingles, Murray, and I need the income from it. The best way to do that was to bring in permanent residents, like your friend, Captain Tanner. These people were obvious choices. They were in the same position as me. For one reason or another, they had no desire to return to England or to be traced here on the Costa del Sol."

Joe kept up the pressure. "And it was that easy to persuade them?"

"I used to sell property. Persuading people is a skill, and I haven't forgotten how to use it."

"The Keeligans? Dimmock? Ann Bamford?"

I sold the place to Maurice Keeligan and Ian Dimmock. Dimmock persuaded Ann Bamford to join us, although I have to admit, I had tried in the past. Ann doesn't like me, but as you're no doubt aware, she likes Ian Dimmock. More than likes."

"And you're saying you knew nothing about what these particular people were up to?"

"Absolutely nothing," Holgate assured him. "Maurice only began fooling around with Pauline after he and his wife moved into Apartmentos Ingles. I had my suspicious about Ann, but I knew nothing of her and Dimmock until he told me Rita was blackmailing him a few months back."

"All good marks for Rita, weren't they?"

Holgate leaned forward and jabbed an angry finger at the air in front of Joe. "You are tarring me with a brush I don't deserve, Murray. All right, so I haven't led quite the upright life I claim, but I repeat, I am not and never have been a blackmailer." He sat back again.

"But once Rita had her claws into you, you ratted on the others."

"Again, you're wrong. I told her nothing of the Olivants nor the Acres. She was a journalist. Despite her denials, her claims to have worked for the broadsheets, she was a hack. She worked for every gutter tabloid in Great Britain during her time. She had ways and means of getting at information, and she wasn't afraid to use it, as you well know. She tried to coerce you within a few hours of your arrival. And she tried it on that friend of yours last year. That gardener. It didn't do her any good, though."

"I know. That's because me and George are by and large, honest, and we're candid enough to tell her exactly what she could do with her information."

Silence fell between the two men, Joe simmering angrily, Holgate looking worried but trying to hide it.

"And ultimately, her knowledge of you lot cost her her life," Joe grumbled.

"The police say it was natural causes."

"There was nothing natural about the cause of her heart attack."

Another silence ensued. This time, Holgate broke it.

"Will you be telling the police?"

Joe rounded on him. "You disgust me. Your pal stole hundreds and thousands of pounds from investors, you paid a blackmailer six thousand to keep her mouth shut, and even now, you don't care, do you? As long as she's dead, you're all right."

The waiter returned with Joe's change. He collected the two, one-euro coins and left the fifty-cents on the tray, pushing it to the waiter.

"*Gracias, señor.*"

"You're welcome, son." Joe watched the waiter amble back to the counter, then concentrated on Holgate again. Pointing at the waiter, he said, "Even he knows what a pleasure it is to earn a few bob by serving others, not himself." Joe stood up and looked at the beaten man opposite with the scorn he would reserve for a stain on his shoes. "You're not worth my time."

He turned, and walked back out into the morning sunshine.

Chapter Ten

"Day off?" Joe asked.

Ann yawned. "No such luck. I have to be at the showroom for three o'clock and if I'm lucky I might be finished for midnight."

After leaving Chico's, Joe had paused on the seafront, watching another sculptor at work. This one had produced a snoozing dragon, similar to a full colour drawing Joe had seen as the front cover of Tolkien's *The Hobbit*.

Many people stopped to take pictures and throw coins into the sculptor's hat, Joe included. He marvelled at the deft touches, made with a few simple tools and the palms of his hand, as the artist fashioned the sand into these wonderful shapes.

He was still admiring it when he found Ann Bamford stood alongside him.

"Clever stuff," she had commented, and Joe readily agreed.

From there it was the most natural thing in the world to ask her to join him for a drink at Pepe's café nearby, where he asked about her free time and she told him of her shifts.

"Not like real work, though, is it?" he said. "You know. It's not physical."

"It's mentally and emotionally draining, Joe," she told him. "You're a businessman. You must know how difficult it is being nice to people you don't really like."

Joe laughed with genuine pleasure. "Nope. I'm not nice with them." He narrowed an intense gaze upon her. "Course, you've had plenty of practice at being nice, haven't you?"

His tone was perfect, signalling bad news; something she would not like to hear. And her face registered it.

"What are you getting at?"

"What is it you used to do in London? An escort? Can't see you escorting prisoners from the Old Bailey to Pentonville or the Scrubs. No, no. Where I come from they're called tarts, or prossies. But in London, it has to be an escort, doesn't it?"

Her face coloured and the bile burned through her words. "How dare you—"

"Speak the truth?" he interrupted. "Tell it like it is? One of my more annoying habits. Y'see, Ann, you know the file you were looking for when you broke into Rita's apartment last night? You were never going to find it. I have it. And it's surprising what it tells me about you. What was your last court appearance for? Soliciting?" He tut-tutted and wagged a disapproving finger at her. "Very naughty. And silly, leaving your calling card in phone boxes. Bound to get you nicked and fined at the very least."

Anger suffused her tanned features. "Now listen to me—"

"As a saleswoman, you should know that the key to controlling situations is to ask questions, not lay down the gauntlet. Right now, I'm asking questions, but I'm not trying to sell you anything. I won't go away, and if you don't answer me, I'll take the entire kit and caboodle to Terrones. It would be interesting to see what he makes of Rita's death in the light of the information I have."

Her shoulders slumped and she played agitatedly with her drink. "I was young. I was broke. I needed the money. And I don't apologise for what I did."

"No, but you don't exactly broadcast it, either," Joe observed. "Listen to me, Ann, I'm not judging you. I don't care what you did in the past. I don't give a toss if you screwed your way through the entire House of Commons. But I do care about what happened to Rita Shepperton, and I don't believe she died of natural causes. I think she was murdered. That's what I think, but I *know* she was blackmailing you, and that makes you a prime suspect for killing her."

"I had nothing to do with her death, and as for breaking into her apartment, I don't know what you're talking about."

Joe shook his head. "That's what I like. Someone who sticks to the script no matter what the diversion." He sipped his cola. "How much was she taking from you?"

Ann's face fell again. "Two hundred a month."

"Pounds?"

"Euros."

"And you just paid up?"

She shrugged. "What choice did I have?"

Joe laughed cynically. "You could have told her to go to hell."

Ann shook her head. "And have her tell my boss about me? Not likely."

"What does it have to do with your boss?" Joe demanded. "It's all in the past. You're earning your living honestly, aren't you? You're a good saleswoman. You get the deal done. What would he have to complain about?"

She tutted. "What century do you live in, Joe?" Leaning forward, with a quick glance around to ensure no one was listening, she went one, "Timeshare has a bad name. It's tainted. Dodgy deals, rigid contracts, high maintenance fees, high pressure sales tactics. The whole of Europe has become determined to distance itself from timeshare, so we have to hide behind new ideas like holiday clubs. It looks good enough on paper, but it's still timeshare when you get down to it. The authorities watch us carefully. They can't be seen to clamp down too hard on companies which provide employment, bring in tax dollars, euros, pounds, or whatever, but tourism is their lifeblood, and they won't do anything to upset the holidaymakers. One whiff of a complaint, one hint of something wrong, and they shut us down. My boss is careful. We all make good money, we have a lot of satisfied customers, but if anyone puts a foot out of line, they're fired. Bear all that in mind and ask yourself, what would happen if the press learned my boss is using a former prostitute as a saleswoman. I can see the headlines now. 'Sign on the dotted line and get laid.' The company would be hung out to dry. So if he learns of it, I'm out on my ear. That way if it does get to the papers, he can say, 'I didn't know, but I fired her when I found out'. It's that simple."

Joe understood and even sympathised with her problem. "Work is no easier to find here than it is in England, is it?"

"It's damned hard," she agreed, "and I have no skills ... other than the obvious ones. I'm too old for working on my back and the Spanish are no more nor less tolerant than the Brits when it comes to flogging your mutton. I've never done any bar work, I refuse to become a cleaner and I don't wanna go back to England. So I shut up about what I used to do, pay the old bat and get on with my job." Her face darkened. "But at the start of every month the commission on my first sale goes to Rita Shepperton. The cow."

"Went to Rita Shepperton," Joe corrected. "She's dead, remember." He, too, leaned into the table. "Everything you have just told me gives you a good motive for killing her, and even if you didn't, it gives you a good motive for breaking into her apartment to find that file."

"I didn't do either," Ann insisted. "If you're looking for a burglar, look at the staff, particularly Juan Pinero. Listen to me, Joe, you have this wrong. Rita was a sick woman. Heart trouble. She could have gone at any time. Ask Maurice Keeligan. He used to collect her prescriptions for her. And she was no spring chicken. I know for a fact she was into her seventies."

"Seventy-two," Joe replied, and smiled at her surprise. "I know more about her, and you, and your neighbours, than you can imagine. And I know about her heart condition. She took a diuretic for it. Made her go to the lavatory a lot. Clear out the salts and other chemicals in her body that would be bad for her ticker. After her heart attack a few weeks ago, she was prescribed low dose aspirin, but you know, Terrones and his people didn't find any in her room. He thinks it's because she never filled her prescription. I think it's because someone took them away and that's what killed her. Miss the odd dose and it could prove fatal, especially at her age. Miss all of them, and she was a definite goner. But for those who knew about her heart condition, it wouldn't take too much to bring on a wobbler. One good argument, one threat of physical violence and she'd be out of here. So don't tell me she died of a heart attack. Tell me what brought it on." He finished off his drink. "I'm not accusing you, Ann. I'm simply saying that like a few others, you had a motive for killing her ... if she was actually murdered. If I can't find out what really happened, then I'll have no choice but to send all the information in my possession to Terrones." He spread his hands. "Beyond that, you, and your chums will be on your own."

"That would be preferable to letting it get to the media."

"Would it?"

"Yes. I know the Spanish police. They wouldn't be that interested."

Joe sighed. "No wonder Juan and his friend call your landing Little England. Terrones and his people are no different to the Met. They're not really interested in an elderly woman with a heart condition which caught up with her. It happens all the time. It happens thousands of times a day in every country in the word. But as you've already said, tourism is the lifeblood of this area and Terrones will be concerned about anything which may threaten that supply line, and murder will threaten it. If he gets one whiff of suspicion, he'll come down on you lot like the proverbial ton of bricks. He will rip you all to pieces to get at the truth, and when he's finished, he'll make a statement to the press to reassure everyone that they can come to Torremolinos without the fear of being murdered in their beds.

And you and your past, and your supposed affair with Ian Dimmock, will get the public airing you're anxious to avoid."

"I haven't had an affair with Ian Dimmock," she hissed. "I haven't had an affair with anyone."

"Really?"

"Really."

"Well, that would be news to Rita. She got the information on Holgate spot on, as well as your past, but that was through her contact in the media. When it came to the tittle-tattle, she was obviously off the mark, because she relied on her own powers of observation, and I know from personal experience that they were lacking." He laughed again. "She tried it on me, you know. First day I arrived, but she was so far off the mark it was idiotic." He leaned back, savouring the pleasant sun. "How did you come to be living at Apartmentos Ingles?"

Ann shrugged. "Ian Dimmock."

"He's your accountant?"

"His partner, Sandra, is," she replied with a nod. "I was living out of town, renting a place in Cortijo de Maza." She pronounced it with a near-perfect Spanish accent. "It was expensive, I had no pool, and I dreaded that journey to work every day. Only about five kilometres, but ..." She drew in a deep breath. "We're all self-employed, you know. Us reps. The company accepts no responsibility for your taxes or insurances, so everyone needs a good accountant. I used Sandra. Not cheap, but a top girl when it comes to getting your tax bill down. When I told her how much I was paying in rent, her eyes almost popped. She told Ian who told me about Apartmentos Ingles. They'd only just moved in. I asked him to make a few inquiries, he introduced me to Holgate and two months later, I had my own place here. I'm less than a mile from the showroom, I have a pool, the beach, even a sea view, bars, restaurants all around me, and I'm saving a couple of hundred euros a month on the rent. Perfect."

"Until Rita got her claws into you."

She nodded. "I knew she was bad news the moment I met her."

"So she was here before you?"

"Before any of us. And we thought we had a good beat on things, you know. We were a happy band of ex-pats living in each others' pockets, and then she started her games. A bad apple who poisoned the barrel."

Joe considered his next question carefully. "Did you know her in England?"

"I knew of her. A scumbag muckraker for the Sunday tabloids. She would sell her soul for a story. She did a lot of undercover work, pulled off any number of stings to expose women like me and the men who bought our services."

"She exposed you personally?"

"No, but I knew one girl who was on the wrong end of her poison pen. She got out of town quick. When I got nicked for the last time, I ran for it, too, before Rita could get at me." Once more, Ann leaned forward to press her point. "She had a downer on the tarts and their clients. It was like a personal crusade."

"Any idea why?"

Ann shook her head. "Only rumours. Her husband got caught with his pants down at an all-night romp where the organisers had laid on escorts for the men. That was the start of Rita Shepperton's campaign against prostitution. She'd been hurt, she didn't care how many people she hurt back. She was a vicious, vindictive harridan. And she hammered both sides of the equation. If the men weren't willing to pay, girls like me wouldn't exist, and if girls like me weren't willing to take cash for services, men like her husband wouldn't have been able to pay for it. It never once occurred to her that if her husband wasn't paying for it, he'd have been jumping some other woman for free."

Determined to avoid the debate, Joe asked, "So when you first moved into the apartments, you recognised her right away?"

"No. Not right away. And anyway, I didn't recognise her, I recognised her name. A few careful questions at the poolside and she told me she was a retired reporter. 'I worked on the broadsheets, you know'." Ann mimicked Rita's high-pitched voice. "Like hell. I knew right away she was lying. She was a hack."

"So let me get this straight. You knew she wasn't who she claimed to be, and yet you didn't use that when she blackmailed you?"

"I tried, but she threw it right back at me. She was guilty of lying, I was guilty of living a lie. Her lies amounted to nothing more than self-aggrandisement, mine amounted to hiding a dirty past. No contest."

"So you paid up."

"So I paid up. I'll tell you something, Joe. I had nothing to do with her death, and as for breaking into her apartment the other night, I don't know what you're talking about, but I don't care. I'm glad she's dead. I can't think of anyone who deserves it more than her."

"Unfortunately, it leaves you with a problem," Joe told her. "Like I said, I have that file, and I have to decide what to do with it."

"Name your price," Ann said. "I'm sure we can negotiate a suitable agreement."

Joe laughed and shook his head. "It doesn't work like that, Ann. Unlike Rita, I can't be bought."

"Joe—"

"There's something about Rita's death that isn't right," he interrupted. "I accept what you and Tom Holgate say about her. She was scum of the worst kind, but that doesn't justify murder. There are legal remedies to blackmail, but none of you were willing to stand up and have your own misdemeanours aired in public, let alone hold her to account for hers. Instead, one of you brought about her death, or at the very least tampered with the evidence, and the rest of you are quite happy to cover for him or her. When I get to the truth, and rest assured, I will get there, then I'll decide what happens." He stood up, ready to leave. "And one last thing, which you can pass on to your chums. I go home on Monday. If I haven't got all the answers by then, it won't stop me working on it, and when I do get the answers, I'll be back in touch with Terrones. None of you will sleep easy until this thing is solved."

He turned and marched away.

***

From the seafront, Joe made his way up to Coyote's and as he expected, found Maurice Keeligan sitting alone outside, reading his newspaper and enjoying the sun.

Ordering drinks, Joe joined him, and at length, Pauline placed a glass of beer before Keeligan and a cola in front of Joe, who handed her the money, took an approving sip and sat back, enjoying the raw, dry heat of the afternoon.

"You're not drinking, Joe?"

Joe shook his head. "Painkillers. Very strong. They don't mix with alcohol."

"Tell me about it. Josie's on some potent stuff."

"So how long have you been out here, Maurice?"

Keeligan smiled fondly. "Five years come November. Josie's idea. Well, you know how bad the weather can be in England. Played havoc with her muscles and joints. It's dry all year round out here, Joe. Oh, we get the odd rainy days, and it can be nippy in January, but it never amounts to much."

Joe nodded sympathetically. "So what is it with Josie? Arthritis?"

Keeligan nodded grimly. "Rheumatoid. The worst kind. There are days when she can hardly open her fists. She'll never be right, but she's better out here than she was back in England."

"Medical bills must be hell, though," Joe commented.

"Not cheap, but not as bad as you might think. She's on a maintenance routine, so we rarely need a doctor. It's prescriptions, mainly." Keeligan smiled again. "But we can afford it. Josie was worth a few bob, you know. Her first husband left her well set up, and I had a few thou put by after I let the trucks go. We're not short, Joe." He sipped the head off his beer. "You thinking of moving out here?"

"Me? Crikey, no." Joe sighed. "I'm fifty-six, I have a healthy business back in England, and I'm not ready to hand it over to my nephew. Not yet, anyway. Lee's a good lad, but I don't think he's ready, either. Besides, what would I do here? Trawl the bars and smoke myself to death?" He patted his pockets, and remembered he did not smoke anymore. "Gasping for a cough and a spit."

Keeligan pushed the pack across the table. Joe reached for it, then declined. "No. I can't. I promised."

Keeligan took a cigarette from the pack and dug into his pockets for a light. "I don't care anymore, you know. They tell me to pack it in, cut it down, then out, and I think, why the hell should I? It's the only pleasure I have left in life."

Joe seized the opportunity. "That and Pauline Wiley's bed."

Keeligan's colour drained. In the act of lighting his cigarette, he paused, the flame of the lighter flickering in the afternoon sun.

"How the hell—"

"Don't pretend you weren't expecting it," Joe advised. "I confronted Holgate this morning and I've just spoken to Ann Bamford. I'm sure they must have phoned you."

Keeligan lit his cigarette and put the lighter on top of the pack. Shifting it to the middle of the table, he drew the ashtray to him and blew out a cloud of smoke.

"How can I put this, Joe? Don't hassle me. Josie might be crippled, but I'm not."

"Neither am I," Joe countered. "And crippled? That's a bit

politically incorrect these days, isn't it?"

"I call a spade a shovel. It's how I am."

"Me too … only I don't. Y'see, Maurice, a spade and a shovel are different things. Similar, but not quite the same. And there's a lot of that about. You telling me about your cosy little life, for instance. It's similar to the truth, but not quite the same. Rita Shepperton's death is another example. The way everyone tells it is similar to what really happened but not quite the same." Joe put a hardened edge in his tones. "I deal with bolshie truckers and even bolshier crumblies every day of my life, so don't threaten me. It won't work."

Keeligan said nothing. His hand shook as he dragged on his cigarette and he refused to look Joe in the eye.

Satisfied that he had the upper hand, Joe went on, "I have the files you were looking for when you went into Rita's apartment."

"I don't know what you're talking about. I haven't been into Rita's apartment today."

"When did I mention today?" Joe asked nonchalantly. "Holgate has been busy, hasn't he? Telling you all about our little tête-à-tête this morning. Now listen. Maurice, it's none of my business what you get up with whom, but I'm making it my business to corner whoever killed Rita."

"Our information is she died of natural causes."

"So it would appear, but when I read what was in those files, I didn't believe it. Each and every one of you has good reason to want to see her dead."

Keeligan sighed, stubbed out his smoke and took a long drink of his beer. "You married?"

"I was. Does it matter?"

"I take it your wife was in good health; not disabled?"

"Fit as the proverbial butcher's dog. Fit enough to leg it away from me when she'd had enough, anyway."

"There you are then. Josie was fit up until a few years back, too, but when the arthritis took hold, it ended whatever, er, fun and games we used to enjoy. I put up with it. You do, don't you? But I'm only human, Joe, and when I had the chance …"

"You took it."

Keeligan nodded. "Wouldn't you?"

"It would depend on the woman," Joe admitted. "All right, so Rita found out and she was blackmailing you. How much and how often?"

"Two hundred a month."

"Pounds?" Joe asked, recalling Holgate's answer to the same question.

"Euros," Keeligan corrected him.

"What makes this information worth two hundred euros a month?" Joe demanded. "Why not tell her where to get off?"

"Because I don't want Josie to know."

"Ah. I get it. Josie controls the money and you're—"

"You're going the right way about finding out how hard I can be," Keeligan interrupted. "It's not about money. It's about not hurting her. She suffers enough as it is without me adding to her pain."

"Forgive me," Joe said, "but I'd have thought the best way of avoiding hurting her would be to keep your zipper fastened."

"What can I say? I'm human. Worse than that, I'm a man."

***

"You didn't tell any of them of your suspicion that she had died elsewhere and was thrown into the swimming pool?" Brenda asked when Joe joined his companions for a cup of tea on the balcony just after twelve noon.

He shook his head. "I want the in-depth on all of them first, so we can work out who was most likely." He leaned on the rail and looked down over the lawns where Holgate held court at a table near the bar. Joe chuckled. "The conclave is in session."

Sheila and Brenda joined him, looking down on the group.

Brenda giggled. "No white smoke, yet."

"White flag more like," Joe responded with a smile.

"They're comparing notes on your meetings, Joe," Sheila guessed.

"Good." Joe returned to the table, and looked out across the sea, into the distance, where a large cruise liner made its slow way into Malaga. "Happy cruisers. Well now that the happy campers here know what Holgate, Ann Bamford and Maurice Keeligan know, they may treat me with a bit more caution, but they'll tell me what I want to know."

The women, too, sat down again.

"They may also decide it's better to shuffle you – and us – off the mortal coil."

Playing with sun glasses, Joe disagreed. "These are not the Mafia, Sheila. How many times have we shoved our noses into murders? All right, so we came close with the Valentine Strangler, and things got a bit nasty in Weston-super-Mare, but most of the time, these people want less attention, not more." Her grinned again. "Besides, we've got Brenda to look after us."

The woman herself, laughed. "Lemme at 'em."

"Seriously, Joe. Who do you think?"

He shrugged. "I don't know. It's not Holgate. He may be a snotty so-and-so, but he's not fit enough to have dragged Rita's body down to the pool. I wouldn't think Olivant or Acre could, either. My money would be on Keeligan or Dimmock or maybe both. Remember, I heard two men arguing."

"You think you heard two men arguing," Sheila corrected him.

"Sheila, I may have been doped up, but I heard two people arguing. I believe they were both men, but I may be wrong about that. Twenty minutes later, you heard Rita's body going into the pool. Knowing what we now know about these people, it's reasonable to assume the two events are connected. I think what I heard was Keeligan and Dimmock arguing about their approach to Rita. Keeligan's wife, remember, has an electric wheelchair. It's the perfect vehicle for getting her from her apartment to the pool, and they're the fittest of the men; the ones most likely to have the strength to do it."

"And the ones with the least likely reason," Brenda pointed out.

Joe concentrated on her, his eyebrows raised, inviting her to go on.

"Keeligan is an adulterer," Brenda explained, lowering her voice to eliminate any possibility of being heard on the balconies either side of them. "That is not a crime. Dimmock, according to Rita Shepperton, is jumping the Bamford bint. That, too, is not a crime, especially since both of them are single. They may have reasons for wanting it kept quiet, but neither of those men is guilty of anything in law."

"No, but both of them had urgent reasons for wanting her shut up; Keeligan because he didn't want his wife to find out, and Dimmock because he's a respected businessman. And besides, Ann Bamford denies any affair with him."

"Sometimes the rumour is enough," Sheila pointed out. "Back home you're a respected businessman, too. Would it worry you if your reputation became a little tarnished?"

"No, but the only people I have to worry about are the Sanford Brewery draymen. I'm not advising clients on how to maximise their tax position. His people will expect him to show impeccable judgement, and if the *real* truth about Dimmock got out, he could be in big trouble." His eyes burned with an intensity designed to will them to believe. "Look at it this way. If word about Holgate and the Olivants got out, the police would investigate. That would take time, and after so long, the evidence may not be that easy to find. They could actually get away with it, despite Holgate confessing to me. Where Dimmock and Keeligan are concerned, the damage would be immediate precisely because they haven't done anything illegal. You see?"

"So in your book that makes them favourite?" Brenda asked.

Joe ticked the items off on his fingers as he spoke. "Two

men heard arguing. They're the fittest, strongest. They had the strongest reasons to want Rita's mouth shut. They're the favourites all right."

"All right, maestro. The ball's in your court. What will you do?"

He smiled at them. "We've been here all week and we haven't seen the centre of Torremolinos, yet. I'm told there's excellent shopping on Calle San Miguel. You up for it this afternoon?"

The women beamed back.

"Great idea," Sheila said.

"Absolutely," Brenda agreed.

"Good. I'm told the Olivants meet with like-minded Christian expats somewhere there, and the Acres favour a small bodega just off the same street." He stood again and leaned on the balcony rail once more, looking down at the group. Holgate and Olivant appeared to be arguing, with the colonel jabbing his finger at the reverend, the way he had stabbed the air in front of Joe. "Right now, I'm dividing to conquer. See? They're arguing now. I have time. Two days yet. I'll deal with them. One by one, and I'll put the fear of God into them. And they'll tell me what I want to know."

Brenda and Sheila chuckled.

"Oy, godfather. Don Murrayonie."

He turned back to look at them. "What?"

"Before you go all Marlon Brando on us, sit down and drink your tea."

Chapter Eleven

The centre of Torremolinos, about 3 km from Apartmentos Ingles, took them by surprise. About a kilometre back from the seafront, there was no hint of a seaside town.

"If you just landed here," Joe said, "you'd swear blind it was any place in any country."

"In Southern Europe," Sheila added, fanning herself against the heat.

The town was a blaze of shopping, little of it linked to the seaside. Tall, modern glass buildings stood alongside older places, and at ground level, the display of goods on offer would rival any large town anywhere. Clothing from cheap to expensive, fancy goods, electrical goods, supermarkets crowded with Friday afternoon shoppers, and the inevitable outdoor bars and eateries leaving the shopper spoilt for choice.

After a cup of coffee at one such establishment, they ambled along the street, protected from the sun by the shade of a small shopping mall, Joe consulting a street map, and on the corner of the mall, they came upon the traffic-free Calle San Miguel.

Turning down the street, it was, as Rita Shepperton had promised, varied and quite cosmopolitan, and they recognised many big names above the shop doorways, mingling with the not quite so well known, and local traders.

Brenda licked her lips in anticipation. "Serious retail therapy," she chuckled. "Just what I needed."

Joe was still looking over his street plan. "Listen, the place I want is right at the bottom of the street." He pointed sunward, where the street narrowed several hundred metres ahead. "Why don't I shoot off down there and leave you two to it. Bell me when you're ready."

"The place you want?" Sheila asked.

"Rita told me the Olivants meet with other Christian people at a café near the church and that's right at the bottom."

The two women disapproved. "Just be careful, Joe."

He dismissed their worries with a grin, and set off down the street, sneaking a few crafty drags, as he went. A hundred metres on, Calle San Miguel crossed another narrow street, traffic permitted on this one, and while he waited for a gap in the line of slow moving vehicles fighting their way through the town, Joe noticed *Bodega Costa del Sol* on the opposite side, a tiny place, wine barrels set on the narrow pavement to act as tables.

Rita Shepperton's words came back to him. "You'll find the Acres at *Bodega Costa del Sol* from about three o'clock every afternoon. They like the local wines."

Joe crossed the street and carried on down Calle San Miguel. It narrowed here, both sides lined with small shops selling souvenirs, cheap clothing and jewellery, standing side by side with the bars and cafés. Many of the places were so crowded out in the sun that they narrowed the street even further, and there was an air of near-festivity amongst the crowds of locals and tourists.

At the very bottom, the street opened out into a small square, with *Iglesia de San Miguel* on the bottom right corner. A small, largely nondescript church, its white walls and large crucifix over the door, nevertheless stood out as a landmark in the busy area, an oasis of peace in the heart of the bustle.

On the right, just before the church, was a large bar, the tables outside crowded, dark clothed waiters scurrying back and forth to fill orders, settle tabs and clean tables. Amongst the people enjoying the hot afternoon sun, he noticed the Olivants.

They were with a group of respectably dressed, but

obviously English, people, and in the middle of a genial, religious debate to judge from the occasional words Joe caught. He strolled across, and while signalling for a waitress, he nudged the Reverend Olivant on the shoulder.

Olivant looked up and his face broke into a smile. "Mr Murray. What a pleasure seeing you here. Shopping with your lady friends are you?"

"They're shopping. I'm sightseeing." He ordered a coke, and took a chair to one side of Olivant and his wife, away from the table of their friends. "To be honest, Reverend, I needed a word with you."

The pair excused themselves and turned their chairs to face him. Joe took his soft drink from the waitress and sipped gratefully on it. "Excellent. Don't go a bundle on fizzy drinks, but in this kind of heat …" He placed the glass between his thighs. "A little bird tells me that of the expats, you've been here longest – apart from the colonel and Rita, that is."

"Five years now," Olivant replied. "Most of the time in Almeria, the last two years at Apartmentos Ingles."

"And not a move we've ever regretted, Mr Murray," Noleen said.

"Of course not. You wouldn't regret it, would you?"

"I'm sorry, Mr Murray. I don't think I understand."

"Oh, I think you do, Mr Olivant. Or should I say Mr Oliver? The Reverend Harold Oliver, vicar of a small parish near Exeter. The same Harold Oliver who disappeared with his wife and thirty thousand pounds from the church restoration fund about fourteen years ago." Joe took satisfaction from the look on their faces. "The same Reverend Oliver who was paying Rita Shepperton every month to keep her mouth shut. The same Reverend Oliver who broke into Rita's apartment two nights ago looking for her files, but didn't find them." Joe smiled. "I already had them."

Noleen appeared shocked, but her husband maintained his aplomb, and looked up. "Forgive this man his wild accusations,

Lord."

"Gar, don't give me that," Joe grumbled. "You and your wife did a runner all those years ago and took money that didn't belong to you so you could fund a new life here. Rita found out about it and threatened to sell the tale to the papers. Difficult for you, that. If the story broke, you'd have the police all over you, and within a month you'd be hauled back to England to pay for your crimes."

"And that is what Rita's information told you is it?" Olivant asked. When Joe nodded, the reverend shook his head and smiled sadly. "Of course, you're right. I was … I still am Harold Oliver even though I introduce myself as Olivant. But Mrs Shepperton did not have the tale quite right, Mr Murray."

Olivant sighed and stared up the street, his eyes vacant, not taking in the crowded bazaars and bodegas. Joe waited. There were times when it was better to be silent.

"We owed a lot of money," Olivant went on. "Credit cards mainly, but there were other debts. We lived in the vicarage, of course, but we had a little holiday home in Torquay. It was paid for and the obvious thing to do was to sell it and settle our debts. But that, Mr Murray, takes time, and we did not have time. The wolves were at the door. So we borrowed from the restoration fund to clear our debts. We believed that the house in Torquay would be sold and we would be able to replace the money before anyone realised it was missing. Then the church auditors paid us a surprise visit."

"So you disappeared?"

"We disappeared," Olivant agreed. "We got into the car and drove off to Portsmouth. We intended getting the Santander ferry and driving down through Spain to this area." Olivant's eyes burned into Joe. "But we never got on the boat."

Joe was surprised. "You didn't?"

"Severe delays due to bad weather in the Bay of Biscay. We had a two-day wait. Two nights spent in a hotel, and during that time, I did a lot of thinking. I had stolen, Mr Murray, stolen money that belonged to the church and had been donated by the good people of my parish. I had stolen from God. I knew I could not run away. I had to stay and face the consequences of my actions. So we got into the car, drove back to Exeter where I handed myself in to the police. In due course, I was tried and sentenced to two years in prison. I was released after one year, I spent the second year on licence, and once I was free to leave Great Britain, we came to the Costa del Sol."

Joe understood. "To avoid the bad press?"

Olivant nodded. "It had taken its toll on my wife, and it would not go away. By this time, of course, the house in Torquay had sold and we were considerably better off so we left Great Britain for a new life in the sun."

Joe tossed the information around in his head. "What I don't get is how Rita could have got it so wrong."

"I told her the truth, and do you know what she said, Mr Murray? Her exact words were, 'what difference does it make'. She abided by the code of tabloid journalists the world over, and refused to let the truth get in the way of a good story."

"So you paid up."

"After some negotiation on the figure, I paid up. You see, I had been punished for my crime by the laws of the land. I saw Rita as God's punishment."

"God's punishment?"

"Do you believe in God, Mr Murray?"

Joe shrugged. "It's not something I stop to think about very often, but my feeling is that when it comes to crime and punishment, God tends to leave it to us mere mortals."

"A mistake so many make," Olivant announced. "There is a reckoning for all our sins, and He will ensure that by our suffering, we will learn."

"And He does that by sending an out and out criminal to punish you?"

"What better way to punish a sinner than by putting him at

the mercy of another sinner? If, as you suspect, Rita was murdered, then she has paid a high price for her wickedness. If, as the police say, she died of natural causes, then she will now be faced with God's judgement. She was sent to teach me the error of my ways in a manner which has, I can assure you, taught me that lesson. And now you have to come to reinforce the lesson."

"Have I?"

"It seems obvious to me that even though I may have learned the lesson, I still have not done enough to atone." Olivant injected a smug note of piety into his voice. "Too many times, I hear people say, 'God help me'. So rarely do I hear people kneel and say to God, 'how can I help you, Lord'. I have not yet offered Him enough service or you would not be here." Obviously satisfied with his analysis, Olivant sighed. "So, Rita took two hundred euros a month from us. How much will you take, Mr Murray?"

Acutely aware that his presence was being monitored by Olivant's friends, Joe suppressed as much of his irritation as he could. "I find your godliness absurd and your final words insulting. I'll tell you how much I want, Reverend. Nothing. Not one penny. But I do want to ensure Rita gets justice. Y'see, as far as I'm concerned, she was a complete toe-rag; a barefaced blackmailer, who should rightly have been punished, and not by God. I leave that to you and your faith. She should have been jailed for her actions. But whatever she did, she did not deserve to die. I can't let that go, and I'm facing a bunch of people who all have a grade one motive for killing her. You talk to me about sin, yet you're here committing the biggest sin of all. Wallowing in your pride. Because that's what this is about. You're hiding away from scum reporters because you don't want to be reminded of your human failing. If you had one ounce of Christian decency in you, you'd want what I want. Justice for Rita. And you wouldn't give a toss who knew what about you."

"Do you know what it's like to be hounded, Mr Murray?"

Noleen asked.

Joe answered promptly. "Yes. Yes, I do. Earlier this year I was arrested on suspicion of murder and the press had a field day with it. But I didn't run away from them."

"Perhaps God saw fit to test you," Olivant suggested.

"Perhaps," Joe agreed. "But I didn't ask Him to help me. I did it myself. I always do. I didn't run away and hide. I faced up to it and dealt with it, and as it happens, I also helped the police pin down the real killer." Joe pointed an angry finger at them. "I have Rita's information and a part of it points at you two. If I can't make sense of this by Sunday, the information goes to Terrones and his people. You ought to think about how you're going to handle the publicity … again."

***

At the rear of a *perfumeria*, while Brenda tested various fragrances, dabbing or squirting them on the back of her wrist and sniffing them, Sheila ambled round the shop and its displays of top name perfumes, her eyes occasionally straying back out on the sunny street.

They had noticed Joe having a crafty smoke as he made his way down the street, and Brenda had wanted to go after him, but Sheila, as she had done previously, stayed her, this time by guiding her into the perfume shop

But Brenda, she reflected, had always had problems making up her mind when it came to buying anything, not just perfume. It was doubly worse here where she was conducting a conversation in pidgin Spanish and noisy English with the proprietor, a wizened, crook-backed woman who appeared to be about ninety years old, and who spoke little English.

"I need something less tangy," Brenda shouted as if the woman were deaf. "You know. Less acidy."

The old woman's eyes lit up. "Ah. *Ácido*."

"Probably," Brenda said chewing her lip. "Sheila, what's the

Spanish for tart?"

"As open to misinterpretation as it is in English, I should imagine," Sheila replied, and glanced through the window again as a familiar figure entered a mobile phone dealer's opposite. "Now what is Juan Pinero doing here? I thought he was working." She called out to Brenda who was now trying a fifth bottle. "I'll just be outside, dear."

"Yeah, right. Won't be long."

Sheila stepped out, and crossed the narrow street. Standing close to the window of a leather goods shop, she leaned to her right, and looked into the phone dealers. Juan stood at the counter, showing a phone to a bearded young man whom Sheila assumed was the shop owner. They were clearly haggling over something. As Juan spoke and the proprietor gesticulated, Juan leaned over and showed the phone, jabbing at the keys, presumably demonstrating its capabilities.

At one point, Juan dropped the phone in his pocket and turned to leave. Alarmed in case he may see her, Sheila concentrated on the handbags in the leather shop, wondering who would be prepared to pay €250 for a small clutch bag.

When Juan did not appear, Sheila again peeked into the phone shop.

The pair were haggling again. The proprietor broke off to answer a query from another customer browsing the handsets hung on the walls, and for a moment, Juan was at a loose end. Leaning on the counter, he half turned and this time, he saw Sheila, and waved a friendly greeting at her.

Irritated that he has spotted her, she nevertheless waved back, and then made a point of studying the phone tariffs displayed in the window. Written in Spanish, she understood less than one word in ten.

When she checked again, Juan and the proprietor had obviously come to an agreement. Juan had decided to take the phone.

To her surprise, however, Juan handed it over, and the

proprietor gave him what looked like twenty euros.

Obviously happy, and quite open about the transaction, Juan stepped out into the sunshine, and beamed on Sheila.

"Señora Riley. Is nice to see you enjoying Calle San Miguel. Shopping is good, yes?"

"Very good, thank you, Juan." Sheila felt uncomfortable."I'm, er, I'm waiting for Brenda; Mrs Jump. She's buying perfume." She waved at the shop across the street.

"Ah, the lovely Señora Jump. She fine lady. You also are fine lady. English roses, two."

Sheila smiled modestly. "So, is it your day off?"

"No, no. I am back at Apartmentos Ingles at four. I have new cellphone." He took out the phone and showed it to her. "I was selling old one to Mario. He drive a hard bargain, Mario." He checked the time on his phone. "I must go. I will see you later, yes?"

Sheila nodded and he strode off up the hill, back towards the town centre.

As he disappeared amongst the crowds, Brenda came out of the perfume shop carrying a tiny gift bag.

"Settled for Chanel," she announced. "How much is forty-six euros in English money?"

Still distracted, Sheila said, "About forty pounds, I think."

"Not bad then; it's about sixty back home … Sheila, whatever is the matter? You look miles away."

"Juan," she replied. "I've just seen him selling a mobile phone."

Brenda shrugged and tucked the perfume in her handbag. "Not a crime is it?"

"What was it Joe said was missing from Rita's apartment?"

"Her laptop."

With a shake of the head, Sheila said, "That was after the break-in. I mean the first time we went there. We couldn't find her phone."

And Brenda, too, turned to look up the street the way they

had come.

***

"This is what Spain is all about, isn't it?" Joe glanced around the dark interior of *Bodega Costa del Sol.* "You won't find anything like this in Blackpool."

After leaving the Olivants in no doubt of his opinions, he had wandered back up the street, wriggling his way through crowds of shoppers, and stepped into the place to catch the end of a flamenco routine, the male dancer, dressed all in black, hammering at the hardwood floor with such rhythm and rapidity that his feet were a blur, while his female counterpart, wearing traditional scarlet, stood by making sweeping, exaggerated gestures.

With the show over, the floor was sprinkled with roses, the dancer's hat passed round, and Joe dropped a few euros in, then joined the Acres in one corner, where they were enjoying a bottle of local red.

They did not appear surprised to see him. It was as if they were expecting him, and when Joe passed his comment on the British seaside, Michael Acre merely smiled. "Blackpool? Lancashire is not an area we're familiar with."

"Hmm. Rough water, the Irish Sea. And you're not familiar with it? Funny that, because according to Rita Shepperton you come from Garstang, which is just up the road from Preston, less than twenty miles from Blackpool."

The Acres exchanged wary glances. "Whatever Mrs Shepperton told you, Mr Murray, she was wrong," Esther insisted.

"Please call me Joe. As I said to Pauline Wiley the other night, it is my name and it's preferable to the names some people call me."

"Very well, Joe. Rita Shepperton told you wrong," Michael said.

"Rita didn't *tell* me anything. Rita left the information behind in her file. The one you were seeking when you broke into her place last night."

"I beg your pardon?" Michael sounded genuinely outraged. "We did not—"

"In fact she left a lot more behind than information on where you lived," Joe interrupted as rudely as he could. "She left the full tale of how you rejected your daughter and how the kid committed suicide a day or two later, and the way the media hounded you for it."

The couple were stunned into silence.

"I have that information now," Joe reminded them. "But what will I do with it?"

Again he was met with stony silence.

"Can I tell you something? I was married for ten years before my wife decided she'd had enough of me and my café, and cleared off to the Canary Islands to live. As luck would have it, we had no children. But I have a great nephew; Danny. He's about four or five years old now, and do you know, I spoil that kid rotten. Between you and me, I love kids. And I wouldn't care if Danny grew up to be mass murderer, I'd still love him to bits. No matter what he does, I will never turn my back on him, and I certainly won't turn him away from my door if he's unlucky enough to get hooked on drugs."

Under the broad brim of his sunhat, Michael's eyes blazed in the dim light. "Well you're not us, are you?"

"Damn right, I'm not. Just looking through Rita's files, most of the British public aren't like you either, judging from the amount of flak you took."

"We have done nothing wrong, Mr Murray," Esther repeated.

"Legally, no. Morally …? Well, that's another debate isn't it? And you obviously feel badly done to otherwise you wouldn't have been paying Rita … how much a month? A hundred? Two hundred?"

Michael sat bolt upright, his back stiff, eyes now glowering. "Is this really any of your business, Murray?"

Joe did not divert his stare. "I'm making it my business, and before you ask why, I'll tell you. Everybody is at pains to tell me that Rita had a heart condition and died of natural causes. She had a heart attack a few weeks ago, and the ticker finally gave out in the early hours of Tuesday morning. I know that there are ways of making that happen, and the more I think about it, the more I see that there is something not quite right about her death. She was dumped in that pool after she died. I know that much. Her apartment was ransacked the night after she died, and I know what the burglar or burglars were looking for. I have it. I got it earlier in the day. Now take those two items, throw in a mob of ex-pats, all of whom she was blackmailing, and it adds up to murder."

"Breaking into Rita's apartment had nothing to do with us," Michael insisted. "That's likely to be a member of staff. They all have pass keys, you know. As for everything else, we have done nothing we are ashamed of," Michael insisted.

"Then why did you feel the need to run from the UK?" Joe demanded. "Why did you feel the need to pay Rita?"

"You said you don't have children, so you wouldn't understand."

"Try me."

Michael heaved a frustrated sigh. "Colonel Holgate warned us about you, you know. He said you had badgered him and you'd do the same with us."

"Did he also tell you that I can't be intimidated and I wouldn't go away?" Joe demanded. "Now tell me what your daughter did that was so wrong?"

"Everything," Michael snapped. "We gave her everything. The best education money could buy, all the extra tuition she needed to help her through her exams, all the financial support she needed when she was at university. Everything. And do you know how she repaid us? She got herself pregnant, hooked on heroin, and she prostituted herself. I lost count of the times I went to court to plead for her. Eventually, I tired of it. She came home, begged us for help and I told her no. Not unless she agreed to move back in and stay there where we could keep a close watch on her. She threw a tantrum, and I threw her out, told her never to come back. Two days later, she was found dead. But it was an overdose. She had not cut her wrists as the more outrageous tabloids reported."

Joe nodded. "A sad tale. I've heard it before, though. Many times."

"I was a wealthy man, Murray. I had my own company. We were doing well. When the story broke, we came under attack, and one by one, the shareholders began to drop off. The order books dwindled until there was nothing in them. We realised our assets and came out here where we could get some peace, get away from those dogs in the media. That's it. That's everything. All we needed was some peace and quiet."

"And then Rita Shepperton found out and got her claws into you. Was she one of the reporters who hounded you?"

"No. If she had been I'd have recognised her right way and we would never have moved into Apartmentos Ingles."

"But she had contacts, didn't she?" Joe pressed. "Ways and means of getting at the information she wanted, and once she had it, she demanded money to keep her mouth shut. How much?"

"Two hundred a month."

"Pounds? Euros?"

"Euros. Sterling isn't much use out here."

Something tried to push itself through the cloud of information clogging Joe's mind. "He dismissed it. "How did you come to be living here, in Torremolinos, in that apartment block? Holgate?"

Esther nodded. "We originally moved into an apartment in San Pedro de Alcántara, near Marbella. It's quite expensive down there, and we were looking for somewhere a little more economical. We bumped into the colonel in a restaurant near Puerto Banus. We got chatting, told him we were looking for somewhere to live, and he said there were free apartments here. We met him again and a third time, then we had a look at Apartmentos Ingles and took it on. It's two hundred euros a month cheaper than San Pedro."

"Which Rita Shepperton took off you," Joe pointed out.

"That only started about a year after we moved in."

"The same as everyone else. Give 'em time to move in, settle in, get used to the others and then ..." Joe drummed his finger on the table. "I'll be frank. People like you annoy the hell out of me. You sat in judgment on a young woman, your own daughter, when she needed your help the most, and now you're having to pay for it. Rita Shepperton, by the sound of it, got exactly what she deserved, but that doesn't make it right, or legal, and it doesn't make it right that someone broke into her apartment and went through it like a dose of salts. I don't know if it was you, I don't care, but I am making it my business to set matters right, and if I have to leave the information with Terrones before I go home, I will." He stood up. "So you two had better be prepared for more flak."

Chapter Twelve

It was getting on for half past four when they finally returned to the apartment, and while Sheila and Brenda prepared an afternoon snack, Joe hurried out onto the balcony with a soft drink and his netbook and brought his notes up to date.

Ten minutes later, the women joined him, bringing with them sandwiches, cakes, and a tray of tea things, and he was compelled to move his netbook to one side to give them some room.

"We need a word, Joe," Sheila said.

"Two minutes," he promised, his eyes focussed on the screen. "And if you're going to lecture me on what I'm doing and what I should be doing, don't. I haven't had a holiday this good in years."

Brenda poured tea for them. "It's not that. We think you may be on completely the wrong track."

He paused a moment, but did not look up from the screen. Instead, he carried on typing, his fingers dancing over the keyboard and even when Brenda put a corned beef sandwich and cake in front of him, he did not pause.

"Well, I must say, that announcement has really gripped him," Sheila announced.

"You can see how astonished he is, can't you? Hanging on our every word."

"If you don't shut up, you'll be hanging off the balcony by your fingertips," Joe warned, still without taking his eyes off the computer.

"By the time you're big enough, Joe Murray, you'll be too

old."

Sheila tittered. "I'll bet you say that to all the boys, Brenda."

By contrast, Brenda guffawed. "And it's true. Most of them aren't big enough, and those that are, always turn out too old."

Joe completed his work, hammered home the final full stop, and saved the file. Carrying the netbook into the apartment, he left it on the coffee table and returned to the balcony, where he picked up his sandwich and bit into it as he sat down.

"Corned beef," he muttered. "You certainly know how to look after a man, don't you?"

"Do you have any idea how expensive it is here?" Sheila asked. "Almost four euros a can."

Joe washed the food down with a swig of tea. "Great. Now I don't know whether to eat it or lock it in the bank for safe keeping." He took another bite. "All right, come on. Tell me why I'm barking up the wrong tree."

Briefly, Sheila ran through her meeting with Juan on Calle San Miguel, and what he had been up to.

"Okay, so you think he may have nicked Rita's phone and that's the one he was selling. Is that it?"

"You've been concentrating on the English residents to such an extent that you may have missed Juan, but when you think about it, he is the most obvious suspect," Brenda said.

"He has a pass key to the apartment," Sheila reminded Joe. "What's to say he didn't ransack the place himself?"

"Some of the Little England crowd are saying the same," Joe told her, "but it doesn't hold together very well. If you recall, the mobile was missing before the break-in. So when did Juan steal it? The night he murdered Rita?"

"Well, that's possible, but I think you're wrong about the murder," Sheila said. "Everyone has said, all along, that its natural causes. You're the only one who won't accept that."

"With good reason," Joe countered. "Rita's pills are missing. Her aspirin. Terrones told me they were nowhere to be found. Listen to me, Sheila, Rita may or may not have been murdered,

153

but she was moved from her apartment and left by the pool. You're now telling me Juan did that. Why? He would have needed help, I'm sure, and there were two men arguing at the time she would have been moved. So he worked with someone else, and all they got out of it was a mobile phone, for which he picked up twenty euros?"

"And a laptop computer, which he stole after the place was trashed," Brenda reminded them.

"And for which he might get another fifty euros. And why didn't he nick the computer the night he stole the phone? Think about what you're saying. Two of them turned up here in the middle of the night, Juan risked his neck twice and all for seventy euros, which will be split two ways? I don't believe it."

"Thieves will work for the tiniest amounts," Sheila assured him. "I recall Peter telling me so."

"I know they will," Joe agreed, finishing the last of his sandwich, "but they're not usually stupid enough to come back to their place of work in the middle of the night."

"He may have taken the phone the morning when the break-in was discovered, Joe," Brenda pointed out.

"It wasn't there when we looked the previous day," Joe said.

"What you mean is we didn't find it," Sheila argued."

"We searched that place pretty thoroughly. If it was there we'd have found it. No, Sheila, that phone was missing when we went in, and if Juan took it, then he was in there before us, and I can't see it. The cops had the place taped off until Wednesday morning. The only chance he had was between the time of Terrones telling us he'd released the apartment, and me asking Juan for the key. Failing that, he must have been in there the night Rita died, and if I'm right about her death, it meant he knew before the girl at the swimming pool raised the alarm."

"All right, then," Brenda suggested, "let's say Juan killed her, or at least had a hand in her death. Was it him you heard arguing on the landing?"

About to begin work on a slice of Madeira cake, Joe frowned. "It's all very hazy. Remember, I'd been drinking and I'd taken my painkillers and antibiotics. But there's a couple of things which make me believe it wasn't Juan. The first man said, 'she won't stand for it'. Won't, not will not. Juan's English isn't the best, and you'll notice that when he speaks to us, he doesn't use contractions. He would have said, 'will not'." He took a bite from the cake.

"And what about the other voice?" Sheila asked.

"He said, and I quote, 'stop griping'. Griping? Juan had problems understanding that by file I meant a computer file, not part of a plumber's toolkit. Hell fire, he even got lips are sealed wrong, didn't he? You're telling me he'd understand the word griping?" Joe shrugged. "I can't be sure who it was, but I'm sure they were English, not Spanish. Either that, or Juan's grasp of English is way better than he's letting on."

"So you're just going to ignore us on this, are you, Joe?"

"No. I think we need to talk to Juan, but my guess is he was telling the truth when he said he was selling his old phone. People do, you know." He finished his cake and washed it down with tea. "We'll get to him in the morning, I think. In the meantime, I have to try and catch Ian Dimmock. He's the only one I haven't spoken to so far."

***

The sun was setting outside Coyote's when Joe finally caught up with Dimmock. Inviting the big man off to one side where they could talk in something approaching privacy, Joe furnished the drinks and Dimmock stared sourly over the top of his beer.

"My turn now, is it, Murray?"

"I left you until last," Joe said. "I figured you'd be the toughest. I also figured that a great deal of the information Rita held on you was wrong."

Dimmock said nothing, but maintained an implacable gaze.

"She had you down for an affair with Ann Bamford. I've spoken to Ann. I know all about her, and her past, and no way would she be in an affair with you. She denies it anyway, and but it would never happen would it? Not because she'd be averse, but she's too low down the scale for a man like you. And yet you paid Rita, so I asked myself if not Ann, then who? Pauline?" He gestured into the bar. "Maurice has her, and she's taking a risk with him. That only leaves Sandra, but she's your partner, so it's hardly Sunday tabloid stuff, is it?"

Still Dimmock said nothing, but stirred his whisky.

"Now if I was as gormless as Rita Shepperton, I'd do a little more investigating on you and come up with nothing, other than what we already know. You're a respected businessman in this part of the world, you don't make a fortune, but you make an above average income. You've been here five years, established yourself as a good, financial advisor, you make good commissions, and one day in the not too distant future, your villa in Marbella will be complete, and you'll leave Apartmentos Ingles."

Joe paused once more and when Dimmock said nothing, he forced himself to remain as calm.

"But I'm not as gormless as Rita Shepperton. I'm smarter than she thought she was. So I didn't run a check on you. I ran one on Sandra Greenwood, and a different picture emerged."

Finally there was a reaction. It was only slight; a narrowing of the eyes to tiny pinpoints. But Joe knew he was getting to Dimmock.

"Sandra Greenwood, accountant, junior partner in Greenwood and Greenwood. The partnership was dissolved some years ago when her senior, who also happened to be her husband, was imprisoned for fraud. He got time off for good behaviour, spent the next two years in England, and then suddenly, he disappeared. So what happened? Did Ian

Dimmock murder Greenwood? No. Ian Dimmock was unheard of until Ian Greenwood disappeared for the simple reason that Ian Dimmock *is* Ian Greenwood."

Dimmock swallowed his whisky. "I've heard enough." He rose to leave.

"Stay where you are," Joe ordered. "Because if you don't, the police are gonna get to know a lot more than they do right now, and that means they will investigate you, and the publicity you're so anxious to avoid will come down on you and blast you out of the water."

Dimmock sat once more and glared unbridled malevolence into Joe's eyes. "Do you know how big a risk you're taking, Murray? I don't jog every morning for the fun of it, you know. I'm twice your size, I'm fit, and known for my ability to look after myself."

"Keep talking," Joe replied. "Fear would make my heart beat a bit faster and that would be good for it. Thing is, I'm not afraid yet." He leaned on the table and fixed Dimmock with his own glare. "I have all the information. If you do anything silly, it goes straight to Terrones, and again, you lose. Now stop playing the big I am and start talking to me."

"I have nothing to say to you."

"You have a lot to say to me. Rita was murdered. I'm sure of it if the cops aren't. Each and every one of you has the motive to kill her. One of you went into her apartment the night before last and ransacked the place looking for the information I have, the information she used to blackmail you all. I've spoken to the others and I can understand why they paid her, but I can't understand why you did. I don't know what you did wrong, but you've been to prison, you've served your time. She had no hold on you, yet you paid her to keep quiet about an affair you never had. If you choose to say nothing, I'll be left to draw my own conclusions and I'll pass them on to Terrones. Y'see, I know about accountants. I have one. He sorts out my VAT returns and my tax. He's a nice bloke, but he nags the pants off me about moving money here and there to take advantage of tax relief. I don't bother. I make a good enough living and when it comes to leaving bequests in my will, I have a thriving business for my nephew. Mine's a cash business, too, so I never know when I'm gonna need to draw on reserves. Now, I'm not saying my accountant is suggesting hooky schemes, but the potential is there, and I have to ask, is that what you're doing? Is that what you did? Could it be that when the British cops nailed you, they only got to the tip of the iceberg? Maybe you'd pulled another million or two from the scam you were running which they never dug up, and maybe you're happy to pay Rita to keep the Spanish cops from opening up your can of worms."

Dimmock smiled. Slowly his smiled turned to laughter. "You're clever, Murray. I'll grant you that. You're smart. You know where to look for answers. But just like Rita, you come up with the wrong ones. Unlike her, you're too dumb to make a profit on what you know."

"I'm not interested in your money, Dimmock. I make enough legitimately."

Dimmock's mirth subsided. "All right. I'll tell you what it's about." He leaned forward again. "I got caught pulling a few fiddles with clients' money. I shouldn't have done it, but I did, and I paid a heavy price for it. Imprisonment was only a part of that price. I was also thrown out of the Institute. That meant I couldn't practice. Not in England, not in Europe, nowhere. Wherever I went in the world, they would ask for references, and once they looked into my past, I would be refused a licence to practice. Fortunately, Sandra could carry on working. She was guilty of nothing and her reputation was never compromised, so we still had a living. Once my sentence was complete, we came out here. It was a risk but it was the only way we would ever get ahead. We managed to negotiate few small contracts. Enough to scrape a living, and while Sandra managed those, I went into the master plan and set myself up as an investment advisor."

"I thought such people had to have a licence, just like accountants," Joe said.

"So they do, but have you seen the exam? So easy, even a thickhead like you could pass."

"Yeah, yeah, yeah. If you wanna annoy me, try bad mouthing my home made steak and kidney pies."

Dimmock ignored the jibe. "Essentially, I'm a salesman. I sell advice. And you know something, Murray, my advice is the best. Some people made a fine profit from it, my reputation began to grow and as it did, other people began to trust me enough to let me move their money around for them. The business is legitimate, it's above board, but I'm an employee of Sandra Greenwood Associates."

"You live under a false name."

Dimmock shook his head. "My name is Ian Dimmock. I changed it by Deed Poll before we left England. Everything about us is perfectly legal, and you've got it all wrong."

"Then why did you pay …" Joe trailed off as the answer dawned on him. "Of course. If Rita thought she had you cornered, she wouldn't investigate you any further."

Dimmock smiled. "Precisely."

"And fifty euros a week, two hundred a month, would be peanuts to you."

"Sandra and I spend more than that on booze," Dimmock agreed.

"All of which means you must be pulling some stunt in the background or you wouldn't give a hoot whether she was investigating you or not."

"Wrong."

Joe said nothing. He merely raised his eyebrows.

"I'm doing well, Murray. I'm making my living entirely honestly, and I'm making a damn sight more than I did sorting out Joe Bloggs Plumbing's VAT and tax returns in the UK. But I ride on my reputation. Can you imagine what it would do to my business if my clients learned I'd served four years for fraud? That kind of problem tends to follow you for life. My clients would run a mile and within a year I'd be left laundering money for the mob."

Joe nodded thoughtfully. "I can see your point. My café runs on the reputation of its food, not service." He laughed. "If they want service with a smile, they don't come to the Lazy Luncheonette, but if they want the best food, they flock there."

"Reputation is vital when you're handling money for others. It's a trust system. They either trust you or they don't, and if they don't, you may as well pack up and go home."

Joe considered the information he had just received.

"All right," he said eventually. "I can see where you're coming from, but I have to tell you, this is bad for you. All of it. You're gonna be investigated and there's a serious danger that everything you've told me will come out."

Dimmock huffed out his breath. "Why can't you just accept that Rita died of natural causes?"

"That would be easy if someone hadn't moved her body."

"You don't know that."

"I do know it," Joe countered. "She did not die in that swimming pol. She was dead before she went into it, and she didn't die alongside the pool as Terrones believes. She died elsewhere. Probably in her apartment, and her body was moved to the pool afterwards. That means someone used the pool to cover something, and as far as I'm concerned, the only thing that needed covering up was the cause of death. I don't know what. I'm no scientist. But I believe her heart attack was induced, and she was dropped in the pool to cover that up. It also means that her body was moved after she died. Now she was no lightweight, so I have to wonder who moved her. You're big, you're fit, you drop right into the frame."

"Wrong, wrong, wrong," Dimmock hissed.

"I've said this to the others, I'll say it to you. Rita was scum, and she deserved punishment, but she did not deserve to die. I go home on Monday. If I can't sort this by then, I'll have no alternative but to hand the information to Terrones, and those of you who were not involved will just have to take your chances that you don't hit the front page of the Brit tabloids … again."

Joe stood, ready to leave.

"You do have a choice, Murray," Dimmock said.

"Really?"

"A one off payment. Cash in your hand tomorrow morning."

"Yours is the second offer today." Joe smiled. "Nice try, but no go."

***

Joe had slept well all week, but with only one day remaining to crack the residents of Apartmentos Ingles, he felt restless and despite going to bed at just after midnight, he could not sleep.

"It's a headache," he had told the women as they sat apart from the residents in Coyote's. "If I go to Terrones with what I have, innocent people are going to be hurt."

"Who for instance?" Brenda demanded.

"Josie Keeligan for one," Joe kept his voice down. "Sandra Greenwood for another. Even Dimmock and the Olivants, both of whom have paid their debt in prison, will be hurt by it. I have to find a way to crack them."

"If you're right, Joe, it strikes me they're all equally guilty," Sheila had said. "They deserve what they get."

"And if it's not a cover up? If it really is just one of them? What then?"

Both women had smiled wanly.

As a result, Joe was up again by one in the morning, moving quietly about the kitchen, making a cup of tea, keeping the noise to a minimum so as not to disturb the women.

He was stirring milk into his tea when all hell broke loose

outside on the landing. Joe could hardly hear what was being said, but he could not mistake the cultured, if frantic tones of the colonel.

Hurrying back to his room, pulling on a robe, he snatched up his key card and let himself out. Next door, Ann Bamford was already out, pulling a wrap round her nightie, and as Joe stepped into the cool night air, Dimmock came from his apartment.

"What the hell is going on?"

"Burglar," Holgate cried. "Caught in my room."

Joe hurried along to the far end, behind Ann Bamford and followed by Dimmock.

"He's in the lift," Holgate cried, frantically waving his arms at the elevator.

Joe paused and looked up at the lights. It was on the first floor, travelling down.

"We'll never catch him," Dimmock said.

"I'll bell reception," Ann said and returned to her apartment.

Joe and Dimmock carried on up to the colonel who, stood in his pyjamas, hair tousled, features alarmed, was the picture of distress. As they ushered him back into his room, Sheila and Brenda hurried along behind.

"Make him some tea, will you, Brenda?" Joe asked as they sat the colonel on a settee.

The old man was frightened and shaking, and it took several moments before he was calm enough to speak.

"I was just nodding off to sleep," he said. "I heard the lock click as someone put a key in it. Came out to investigate, and he was here. In my room. Looking through my cupboards. Naturally, as soon as he saw me, he pushed me out of the way and ran for it. Typical Spaniard."

"Spaniard?" Dimmock asked.

"It was Pinero."

Joe and Sheila exchanged cautious glances.

"Juan?" Sheila asked. "You're sure?"

Brenda came from the kitchen and passed the distressed man a cup of tea.

He sipped at it. "Only got a fleeting glance in the dark, as he ran for it, but it was him. I'd know him anywhere."

Joe paced the apartment floor. "I don't get this. Why would Juan break into your apartment? What was he after?"

"Not much to steal," Brenda commented looking around.

"It depends how you define value." Dimmock said. "Juan is a local, isn't he? He'd know local people. People he could sell things to, trinkets, electronic equipment, that kind of stuff."

Joe, too, looked around. He could see nothing much of the kind of thing Dimmock was referring to. "You keep much in the cupboards, Holgate?"

"Sorry, Murray." Holgate gestured at the table and an ornamental fruit bowl on it. "Would you pass me my hearing aids, please, Mrs Riley?"

Sheila handed them to him and he fussed for a moment, setting them in his ears and checking they were working.

"Now, what did you say, Murray?"

"Nothing," Joe said. "Doesn't matter."

Ann appeared at the door. "Gone," she said. The night manager was probably asleep, but he says he hasn't seen anyone."

"Typical," Holgate sneered.

"Not much we can do now, is there?" Dimmock said. "Will you be all right on your own, Tom?"

"I should think so. He's hardly likely to come back, but I'll bolt the door just in case."

"I'll call Terrones for you first thing in the morning," Joe offered.

"I don't think that will do much good, Murray," Holgate said. "They all stick together, and without one of you seeing him to back me up, I doubt that Terrones would believe me."

"As you wish. Well, you know where we are if you need any

more help."

Joe escorted his two companions back to their apartment.

"That's a turn up for the book," Brenda said, as Joe let them in. "Looks like you were wrong after all, Joe. It is Juan."

Joe laughed. "You think so?"

"Well, don't you?" Sheila asked.

"I think, Sheila, that this little show was well-timed, and perfectly performed, and it was put on purely for our benefit." He locked the door behind them.

"What?"

Joe nodded. "It was faked. All of it. And it was designed to persuade us that they're all innocent while the evil Spanish are getting their own back for us sinking the armada."

"And you're certain of this?"

"Absolutely."

"You can prove it?" Brenda demanded.

"Not only can, but will. First thing tomorrow morning, I'll call a council of war and bring everything to a head."

Chapter Thirteen

Familiar by now with the morning routine of the residents, Joe was making his way to the supermarket at eight thirty on Sunday morning, when he intercepted Dimmock on his return from his early jog.

"Get your people round the pool. Ten o'clock."

"Why should I?" Dimmock demanded.

"If you don't you'll all be running from the media in a few days."

Joe did not wait for Dimmock to respond, but carried on his way to the supermarket.

After returning, he and his companions sat out on the lawns, and as soon as he spotted Juan, Joe called him over.

"Sit down a minute, Juan."

The janitor looked nervously around. "Señor Murray, my boss, Christobel, if she sees me sitting, talking to guests when I should be working, I get fired."

"You leave your boss to me," Joe told him. "If she has anything to say, I'll put her straight. I need to talk to you, and right now, you have more to worry about than the sack."

"Sack? What is this sack I need to worry about?"

"Just sit down, lad."

Reluctantly, Juan sat facing Joe, who leaned forward and kept his voice down.

"We're talking about the death of Rita Shepperton and the way her apartment was trashed. Yeah?" Joe waited for Juan to nod his understanding, then went on. "Most of the residents say you did it."

Juan snorted. "This is no surprise to me, señor. The residents, they do not like me. It is because I am Spanish and not English. They do not like me, they do not like my cleaners, they do not like my boss, Christobel. They do not like anyone if they are not English."

"I understand that, son, and I'm sorry. All I can say is most Brits are not like that. But, we do have a problem because whoever went into Rita's apartment had a key. You remember we agreed that. As far as I can work out, you're the only one with a key to that apartment."

"No. No, señor, is not true. I have no key. Every day when I finish work, I hand my key to Christobel, and I take it again when I come to work the following day."

"So Christobel would know if your key was not handed in on Wednesday evening?"

Juan nodded. "Is security. The keys are checked every day when I finish work. Is a pass key, *si*? With this key I can enter any apartment in the building."

"What about the cleaners?" Joe asked. "Do they all have pass keys, too?"

"*Si, señor*. Every day they must sign out for their keys, and every afternoon, they must hand them back and sign the book. Christobel, she has to sign, too."

"To say that she's received the keys?"

Again Juan nodded and Joe fell silent, considering the information. "How difficult is it to make the key from a blank?"

Juan's face became blank. "*No entiende*. I do not understand."

Joe tutted. "How do they make the keys?"

"Ah, I see." Juan considered his words. "Christobel, she has the cards, *si*? They open nothing."

"They're blank."

"Ah, now I understand you. Yes, they are blank. When a new key is needed, she does work on the computer and it makes the key."

"There's probably a special set up for pass keys, Joe," Brenda suggested.

"This is so," Juan agreed. "Keys can be made for any apartment, or they can be made for all apartments."

"And who has access to the computer?"

"Only Christobel and her colleagues, the other managers for night shift and days when Christobel is not working."

"So if we checked with Christobel, she would confirm that all the keys were handed in on Wednesday evening?"

"*Sí.*"

"Well before we get to that, you met Mrs Riley in Torremolinos yesterday. Remember."

"Of course, I remember. I am not stupid, señor."

"Just keep it calm, Juan," Joe advised. "Now, we all know that Mrs Shepperton's mobile phone is missing along with the computer. The theory is you stole both, and that the mobile phone you were selling in Torremolinos yesterday was Rita's."

"Pah. Is nonsense. You think I want that old thing she used? Mario, he would give me nothing for it. I say to Señora Riley, and I say to you, I was selling my old phone because I have new one." He dipped into his pocket, came out with the phone and tossed it to Joe. "Samsung Galaxy. Best phone on market. No? I surf web, I make football scores, I check TV and I even read books. Is brand new. I got it only last week. Señora Shepperton's phone? Nokia wind up with key. Like a toy."

Joe chuckled. "No street cred?"

"She can phone, she can make text, but nothing else. Worth maybe one euro but only to the man who is hard up." Juan sneered. "If I were to steal, I would not steal this, and you hurt me by saying I steal it."

Joe handed the phone back. "No offence, Juan. I was sure of you, but we're trying to work out what's going on here, and I had to ask, if only to clear your name." He stood up. "All right. Let's go check with Christobel on these apartment keys."

Juan's irritation quickly disappeared. "But, señor, if you say this to Christobel, she will know that I did not report the matter and you will get me into trouble."

"Leave her to me. You won't be in any trouble."

Joe was almost wrong. When told of the situation, Christobel was not only angry, but determined to call in the police.

"You have encouraged Juan to commit a crime, Señor Murray. I cannot permit that. Apartmentos Ingles has a reputation and it is my responsibility to keep it up. And anyway, and if I do not report the matter, then I am as guilty as him." She waved a hand at her errant janitor.

"All right, let me run this past you, Christobel. How would it suit Apartmentos Ingles' reputation as the place where a major crime took place, continuously for a year, right under management's collective nose, and they did nothing about it?"

Shock crossed her face. "I do not understand."

"I know you don't. Juan, here, doesn't understand, either. Neither do my two friends, Mrs Riley and Mrs Jump. But that doesn't change a thing. Rita Shepperton was a criminal, and she carried out her crimes over the last year while she was living here. All I'm trying to do is keep it quiet until I can get to the bottom of it, and then you can call Terrones. That's all I was trying to do when I asked Juan to shut up."

"But what is this crime?" Christobel demanded.

"Blackmail. And it's possible that Rita was murdered because of it."

"Murdered?"

Joe nodded slowly to ensure the full import of his suspicion sank in.

"Then there is even greater need to call Inspector Terrones?"

"I tried to tell him but he doesn't believe it," Joe explained. "Rita apparently died of natural causes. I think differently, because I know so much more about her than he did." He leaned further over the counter. "Listen, all I'm asking is that you give me a day or two to sort it out. If I can't, well I'll go to Terrones with what I know, before I go home. Come on, Christobel, we both want the same thing. Just keep it under your hat until tomorrow morning. Yeah?"

She took a long moment to come to a decision, but eventually, she nodded. "Very well. I will say nothing for the moment, but I must know that the police have been informed before you leave tomorrow, or I will report the matter."

Joe smiled broadly. "Good girl. You know it makes sense. And remember. This was none of Juan's doing. If you're going to blame anyone, you blame me. Now, on Wednesday, did all the staff hand in their pass keys before they went home?"

"One moment."

Christobel made a great show of ducking under the counter, coming up with a loose-leaf A4 binder, and checking the sheets inside.

"Yes," she said eventually. "There were no keys unaccounted for."

"Good." Joe turned to leave, but Sheila stopped him.

"Just a minute, Joe." She faced the receptionist. "Christobel, do the staff ever lose pass keys?"

Christobel threw her hands in there air. "Do they? They leave them in the rooms, they throw them in the waste bins, by accident, of course. Sometimes it is two or three keys in a week. Other times, they are careful and we go many weeks without losing one."

Sheila smiled. "Thank you."

They came away from reception.

"Why so smug, Sheila?" Joe asked.

"I'm happy to accept that Juan was telling the truth, but anyone could have one of those keys, Joe. It doesn't have to be the seventh floor residents."

"No. But they're still the favourites."

***

169

As Joe anticipated, all the residents but Josie Keeligan were there when he, Sheila and Brenda joined them after collecting drinks from the bar.

Joe sipped his soft drink and looked around his audience. "It's time to bring matters to a head," he declared. "For obvious reasons, Maurice, your wife is left out of it. First let's clear up one or two points. I'm British, just like the rest of you, but there are times when I'm ashamed to admit it. Especially when I have to lump myself in with people like you."

Dimmock bristled. "You've been told everything, Murray, so don't get on your high horse about us running out on dear old England. We all had our reasons."

"That's not what I'm talking about," Joe replied. "I'm talking about your blatant racism and your efforts to railroad Juan, a decent, hard working lad, last night."

A mutter of discontent ran round the table.

"But he doesn't matter to you, does he? He's just a Spanish lackey, there to jump at your command, convenient when you need a scapegoat."

"He attacked me," Holgate said. "I will testify before any court that it was him. He broke into my apartment and when I challenged him, he pushed me aside and ran for it. The coward."

"And you're the biggest conman of the lot, Holgate," Joe sneered. "It wasn't Juan, and you know damn well it wasn't him. The only questions I can't answer are how many of you were involved in that little sham and who was it supposed to fool? Me or the cops?"

More murmurings ran round the table and Holgate put on a show of outrage.

"How dare you—"

Unimpressed, Joe interrupted. "Let's run through what happened again. You were in bed, you heard the lock on the door click, got up to investigate, and you were pushed out of the way as Juan ran past you to escape."

"Correct," the colonel snapped. "And don't you tell me it wasn't him. I'd know him anywhere, even in the dark."

"But how could you hear him? Your hearing aids were in that silly fruit dish on the table."

A shocked silence engulfed the table.

"You couldn't hear me when I asked if you kept much electronic gear in the apartment. You asked Sheila to pass your hearing aids over. So how could you hear the lock clicking open, especially considering you were in bed, presumably nodding off to sleep?"

Holgate's mouth fell open and his face coloured. Joe noticed that the others sported various expressions from shock, to worry, to disgust, the latter aimed at Holgate.

Joe leaned forward, jabbing his finger into the tabletop to press home his point. "I've never worn hearing aids, so I don't know how bad they are, but if they're anything like the little earplugs you get with an mp3 player, they'll be uncomfortable. Are you seriously asking us to believe you sleep with them in? And if you do leave them in, do you expect us to accept that even though you'd just been attacked, you took them out and placed them carefully in the fruit dish before tackling the intruder or crying out for help? It was a set up and you know it. You carefully disarranged your room, then came out onto the landing and called the lift. And when it arrived, you pressed the button to send it back down, got out quickly, ran back to your door and shouted for help. By the time we came running out, the lift was near the ground floor, and you were playing your part."

"All right, Murray," Dimmock said. "You've made your point."

Joe turned on him. "So you were involved, too?"

"We were all involved," Dimmock admitted. "It was designed for your benefit, and yes we were throwing suspicion on Juan, but deservedly so. You've been looking for the person who ransacked Rita's apartment a few nights ago, and it had to

171

be Juan."

"Why? I mean—"

The colonel cut him off rudely. "Ask yourself, who had a pass key to that apartment. Pinero, that's who. What was missing? A laptop. And who would know the right people to sell a stolen laptop to? Pinero."

Joe waited to see if there would be any more. When there was not, he said, "You all believe that Juan Pinero entered the apartment?"

A general muttering around the room left him in no doubt.

"I see. Well, obviously, I've misjudged you. I thought you were simply desperate, but now I see that you're really stupid. All of you."

More protests erupted, but Joe rode over them.

"You obviously believe that I and my friends never thought of Juan. It never occurred to us that he had the pass key and if anyone was likely to know buyers of hooky machinery like a laptop, it would be him."

"You can't be expected to know everything, Murray," Dimmock commented. "You've been here less than a week. You don't know Pinero like we do."

"Of course not." Joe put on what he imagined was a thoughtful expression. "It's odd, though. Y'see, I did know Juan had a pass key. That's how I got into the apartment before it was trashed. It's how I got hold of the files before you lot."

"Now listen, Murray—"

This time Joe did the interrupting. "Juan knew that I'd seen the inside of the apartment. Why, then, would he have invited me back to show me that it had been burgled."

"Because he's that stupid," Alice Olivant suggested.

"I see. On the one hand he's smart enough to spot the goodies that Rita possessed, and clever enough to come back here at night, dodge the concierge, get into the apartment and nick them, but on the other, he's so dumb he lets me in to see the apartment after it's been burgled—"

"Listen—"

Joe rode over another attempted interruption, this time from Maurice Keeligan. "Despite knowing that I'd be going home in a few days, he couldn't work out that the simplest course of action was to keep his mouth shut until I'd gone. He came to me with this burglary, and to be frank, he is simply not that stupid. If he were guilty, he would know that it would raise my suspicions." Joe shook his head at them. "Now let's lay it on the line, eh? Juan did not have a pass key to get into Rita's apartment. We checked and his key was handed in when his shift finished. It wasn't Juan. It was one of you."

"That," the colonel hissed, "is libel."

"I think you'll find it's slander, not libel," Sheila corrected him, "and it's only slander if it cannot be proved."

Holgate gawped, others looked away. Only Dimmock held Joe's gaze. "Can you prove it?"

Joe shrugged. "Not quite. But I will. And what the hell, even if I'm wrong, you're not going to the cops, or even your lawyers to sue me, because if you did, I'd have to put the information at my disposal into their hands." He smiled evilly. "I'm sure none of you wants that."

Holgate blustered, others looked angry but none, it seemed, were prepared to call Joe's bluff.

Sandra Greenwood smiled upon him. "Mr Murray, what would it take to get you to see reason?"

"Whatever it is, you haven't got it," Joe said as offensively as he could. "As far as I'm concerned, I am being reasonable. I'm sitting amongst a group of people who know more than they're letting on and that grates."

"How about ten thousand euros?" Sandra asked.

Joe stared at her for a long, angry moment, then turned to Sheila. "You see reason a lot better than me. Money in those amounts blinds me. You tell them."

Sheila cleared her throat. "You obviously don't understand. Any of you. Neither Joe, Brenda nor I are interested in money.

We're not on a witch hunt, but we cannot be bribed. Please don't offer again, because you'll only make Joe angry and when that happens, he's likely to do something silly."

"Like what?" The challenge in Keeligan's voice was quite clear.

"Like go to the cops with what I have," Joe retorted. Once again he leaned on the table, stressing his superiority over them. "The only reason I haven't seen Terrones is because I don't want to put the innocent amongst you through the mill. I know what went on. I just don't know who did it. But I do know that there was more than one of you involved."

Dimmock reacted angrily. "What the hell are you talking about?"

"I mean this whole thing." Joe waved wildly around them. "A carefully engineered plan to make it appear that Rita Shepperton died by the pool and fell in. It couldn't be done by one person. There were at least three of you in on it. I want to know which three."

Bedlam broke out around the table attracting the attention of other guests enjoying the sun on the lawns.

Joe waited for calm. "It was unfortunate for you that Rita chose this week to die; the very week that Yorkshire's best detective was staying here."

Michael Acre frowned. "Yorkshire's best detective?"

"Me, you idiot," Joe said with great affront. "Ask anyone. Ask Sheila and Brenda. Ask Les Tanner if you're all still here the next time he visits. There's no one better than me when it comes to noticing things. Whoever worked this out was good, but there were inconsistencies that took a bit of explaining. They were tiny things which most people wouldn't have noticed, but I did notice them and they let the plan down." He rounded on the colonel. "Rita phoned you as she was dying. In fact, you were the only one Rita could phone because your number was the only one on her computer. And why was it there? Because you'd had an affair with her when she first came out here. When you found her dead, you should have called the cops, but then an idea occurred to you. If you could move her body, the police wouldn't search her flat too thoroughly, and it would leave you the opportunity to go back later and search for the files, the information she had on you. So you called on others, especially Dimmock and Keeligan, the only two men who would be capable of lifting her into Josie Keeligan's wheelchair. Because that's show you got her down to the pool." He swung his attention on Maurice. "The argument I heard, and which I assumed was two victims arguing about an approach to Rita, was actually you complaining that your wife wouldn't stand for someone using her chair."

Keeligan looked away, and so too did Olivant.

"Murray, you're talking absolute nonsense," Holgate declared.

"Am I? One of the things I mentioned to Terrones was how wet the lounger was. He believed Rita had had a swim and then been resting on it, but I knew differently." He aimed an angry finger around them "You set Rita's body on the lounger, tipped it over to roll her into the pool, but one of you let go and the lounger fell in, too. That was the noise Sheila heard and that's how it got soaked."

Worried glances passed between several people. Joe noticed that neither Holgate nor Dimmock appeared unduly concerned.

"Terrones insists that Rita died a natural death. I don't think she did. I think she was murdered and that some of you were involved."

His announcement was greeted by another howl of protest, but once again, neither Holgate nor Dimmock joined in.

When everyone had settled again, Dimmock laid calm eyes on Joe. "You can't prove anything, Murray."

Joe was more than ready for the objection. "How many times have people said that to me in the past? Too many to count. Well let me tell you something, Dimmock. I don't have to prove it. I don't have to prove anything. All I have to do is produce evidence – which I can – and that will be enough to provoke an investigation from Terrones, and during the course of that investigation, these dirty little secrets you're all hiding will come out. Terrones knows nothing of them yet, but you all know they're enough to put him on track."

His announcement was greeted with concerned silence. It was Dimmock who recovered and reacted with uncharacteristic vehemence.

"What the bloody hell do you want, Murray? You were just offered ten thousand for those files and you turned us down. What do you want? A monthly deal like Rita had?"

"And you were told what I want, Dimmock. Justice for Rita. She was a crook, but she did not deserve to be murdered."

"She was not murdered," Dimmock snapped.

"How do you know? Were you stood in front of her when she died?"

"Of course not."

"Then don't tell me—"

"Take my word for it, Murray," Holgate interrupted. "Rita died of natural causes. I know. I was the one who found her."

Chapter Fourteen

In the silence that followed Holgate's announcement, Joe turned his angry stare on the colonel. "Go on."

"She rang, as you guessed. I had my hearing aids in. I can't hear too well on a mobile phone with them. All I heard were a few strangled gasps and it sounded as if she were saying 'tell me'. By the time I took my hearing aids out, I could hear nothing. That was when I realised she was actually saying, 'help me'. So I went round there right away."

"Because you have a key to her apartment, don't you? From the days when you and she were an item."

"Yes. I knocked and rang the bell, and when I got no answer, I let myself in. I found her on the living room floor. I promise you, she was dead when I found her."

A sombre silence fell over the table. Joe noticed that they would not look at each other.

"What time was this?" he asked.

"About half past four in the morning."

"And you didn't call the cops right away?"

"We'd had contingency plans in place for a month, Mr Murray," Esther Acre told him. "Ever since Rita had her heart attack."

"On her death, we would search her place and find the files she had on us," Olivant reported.

"But we didn't expect it to happen in her apartment," Holgate said. "We all thought she would die in hospital. The original plan was, if and when she went into hospital again and died, we would search the place for the files."

Joe frowned. "Why not take them while she was in hospital for the first heart attack?"

"How could we?" Dimmock demanded. "We knew she'd be coming back. Think about it, Murray. She told Paul Wiley about his wife and your friend last year for no other reason than she couldn't profit from the knowledge. We couldn't risk her doing the same to us, and we knew that when she came home, she'd realise the files were missing and blow the whistle on us out of sheer spite."

The explanation sounded reasonable to Joe, and he nodded. "But you knew she would have a second heart attack fairly quickly, didn't you, because one of you stole her pills."

"Utter nonsense," Holgate argued. "We had an idea she would have a second one, yes, and that it would probably kill her, or leave her so ill that she wouldn't have long to go anyway. We didn't have to take her pills, Murray, because she was so hopeless at taking them. She missed dose after dose of her diuretics, which is what caused the first heart attack."

"It's perfectly true, Joe," Maurice Keeligan put in. "I used to collect her prescriptions, so I know. They were supposed to be filled once a month, but she could go six to eight weeks between them."

"Then what happened to her aspirin?" Joe demanded, and was met with silence.

"Eventually, she died in her apartment," Dimmock went on, "And when that happened, we knew that the police would look round the place. Because of the early hour, we didn't have time to search for the files before the cleaning staff arrived for their day's work."

"So you moved her?" Joe looked to Dimmock and raised his eyebrows. "And you were all involved?"

Dimmock nodded. "Holgate called me, I got the others up. Maurice brought his wife's chair after some debate, which was the argument you heard. Sandra and Noleen dressed Rita, Maurice and I manhandled her into the wheelchair and as you surmised, we took her down to the pool. Ann kept the night manager talking while we sneaked her out through the poolside doors to the lawns."

"And I was right. One of you dropped the bloody lounger into the pool along with her."

"She was heavier than I expected," Acre said. "Maurice had to get his wife's chair back quickly, so I helped Dimmock but I let go of the lounger as we were tipping it, and it, sort of followed her into the pool."

A smug smile crossed Holgate's features. "So you see, Murray, we were guilty of nothing."

Sheila, who had been quietly fuming alongside Joe, allowed her anger to flood. "Oh yes you were. You moved a body from the scene of death. At the very least that could be construed as tampering with evidence. I'm certain the Spanish police wouldn't take too kindly to it."

"We were trying to protect ourselves, Mrs Riley," Keeligan pleaded. "Is that so wrong?"

Sheila bristled. "Covering up a death, suspicious or not? Moving a body? Breaking into the dead woman's apartment and ransacking it? Yes, Mr Keeligan, it is wrong."

Keeligan shrank back into his chair under her anger. Holgate was made of sterner stuff.

"No one broke into Rita's apartment, Mrs Riley."

"No. You used your key," Joe countered. "But you still ransacked the place. Why? To try laying the blame on the staff here?"

"We were still looking for the files, as well you know," Ann Bamford grumbled. "We didn't know you had them at the time or we wouldn't have gone back in. Ian has already told you, we didn't have time the night she died, and the night after Terrones removed the police tape from the apartment door was the first opportunity we had after her death. And the reason we didn't tidy up was because we ran out of time ... again. We were at it for hours, and the cleaning staff were due in ...

again. We had to get out."

"Obviously, you hadn't banked on one of the maids going in there by accident and discovering the mess you'd left."

"Accident, my foot," Holgate snapped. "She's like all these people. An eye on the main chance. She was looking for what she might be able to steal."

"You're a fine one to talk," Brenda said.

"The information in those files was ours," Holgate bridled.

"Wrong," Joe told him. "The information in those files is in the public domain, and the actual files belonged to Rita Shepperton. You have no more right to them than anyone else, so you're still guilty of breaking and entering with intent to steal."

"You stole them," Dimmock objected.

Joe smiled slyly. "No. I took them for safe keeping until I could hand them over to the police."

A stony silence followed. Eventually, Holgate broke it. "Well now you know everything, Murray. You know we're not murderers. In fact we're more the victims in this farce. So what —"

"Victims?" Joe almost exploded and Sheila had to order him to calm down. "Let me tell you something, Holgate. I've spent my life running a small business, and I've never stolen anything from anyone. I run a large club for the benefit of its members. I handle anything up to a hundred thousand pounds a year in club funds, and I've never taken a penny from it." He glared at Keeligan. "I was married for ten years, and it was a crap marriage, but I never once took to another woman's bed while Alison and I were together. I may be a grumpy old sod, but at least I'm honest and I own up to it." Next under the steely glare were the Olivants. "I don't hide behind religion, I don't try to excuse myself because someone close to me is disabled and I don't try to hide the things I've done wrong in my younger days. Don't talk to me about victims." He stood up. "I'm never one to take advantage of another's demise, but when Rita

Shepperton died I thought it might give me the opportunity to take over her lease, give me somewhere pleasant to come to when the stress gets too much back home." He glowered at them. "But I've changed my mind. I wouldn't want to live in the same town, let alone next door to any of you." He marched away towards the bottom gate.

The residents stared glumly after him, Sheila with more concern.

Brenda stood and spoke to her best friend. "I'll go after him. Calm him down."

***

Joe was trudging across the sands by the time an out-of-breath Brenda caught up with him.

"Slow down and calm down, Joe. Sheila's told you once, getting angry like that won't do your heart condition any favours."

He half turned to scowl at her. "I don't have a heart condition. I have a pulled muscle."

"Yes, Joe, but you don't know which muscle, do you? And you don't know that you don't have a heart condition either. You won't know until you've had your scan. Just calm down." She linked her arm through his. "We didn't bring you all this way to get annoyed over that bunch of ... of ..."

"Tossers?"

"A bit crude, but probably accurate. They're little Englanders, Joe. Wallowing in their isolation and superiority."

"Assumed superiority," Joe corrected her. "You know, they deserved Rita Shepperton. All of them."

"Yes. I know. But you don't deserve to make yourself angry and ill because of them."

They moved to the water's edge and took in the sun beaming from high in the sky. Brenda felt Joe take several deep breaths, letting the peace and serenity of the area wash over him.

"It's beautiful here, isn't it?" Brenda said.

"And what have we got for tomorrow? The cold and the rain in Sanford."

"If you didn't have the downs, Joe, you'd never appreciate the ups, would you?"

"I suppose not."

They stood silent for a moment. Joe watched a large, cruise liner as it departed from Malaga twenty miles up the coast.

"What will you do with the files?" Brenda asked.

He shrugged. "I don't know. I should give them to Terrones, but like I said, some people would be hurt by the revelations; people who don't deserve to be hurt."

"Josie Keeligan and Paul Wiley?"

"Hmm. Yeah. Ann Bamford and Sandra Greenwood, too. Ann's past is her past, and she doesn't deserve to be fired for it. Sandra was a victim of her husband's greed. He's paid his debt to society and it's right that no one should trust him, but she never did anything wrong." A deep frown etched itself into his brow. "There's something just not quite right, though."

Brenda chuckled. "Come on, Joe, let it go. You cracked the case. There was no murder involved, but there was a lot of scheming and plotting afoot and you uncovered it."

Joe shook his head. "You know me, Brenda. When I tell you there's something not right, I mean it. Something is niggling away at me. Something about those missing aspirin. It doesn't quite fit, and it tells me that the whole picture is slightly out of focus."

"You've answered all the questions, Joe. You've forced them to back down, admit what they did. All you have to decide is whether you're going to tell Terrones, keep the files yourself or hand them over to one of the more level-headed people in the group: Sandra or Maurice."

"What would you do?"

Brenda considered the question. "I wouldn't bubble them to

the law, because they're not evil or wicked. Conniving, certainly, scheming, definitely, hypocritical, too, but they were trying to protect themselves. Watching their backs. Personally, if I was in your position, I think I'd keep the files, make them sweat, really punish them for the way they've behaved and then, when I got home, I'd destroy them … the files, I mean, not the people."

Joe smiled crookedly. "We'll see. Come on. Time we were putting the wind up them again. It'll give me an appetite for lunch."

"What are you going to do?"

"First thing they can do is tidy Rita's apartment up. After that, I'll decide."

Chapter Fifteen

Pushing the ice cream dish away for her, Brenda wiped her mouth on a napkin, sat back in her chair, and patted her belly. "That," she declared, "was delicious."

Joe, too, sat back, replete. "Do you know what would help this meal go down? A cigarette."

Sheila giggled and Brenda wagged a semi-serious finger at him. "No you don't, Joe Murray. You are not going to wind me up." She signalled their waiter.

"*Si, señora?*"

"You have been looking after us all week, young man," Brenda declared. "What's your name?"

"Rafael. My friends, they call me, Rafa."

Brenda reached for her bag. "Well, Rafa, it's time for me show my appreciation." She took out her purse and opened it. Fishing into it, a frown crossed her brow. "Oh, dear. I've only got English money." She smiled up at Rafael. "We're going home tomorrow. Sheila, lend me ten euros will you until I can get to a cash machine."

With a broad smile, Joe dug out his wallet. "Here. I'll see to it." He opened the wallet, and checked the compartments. In the back were several euro notes, and in the front, about a hundred pounds sterling. He fished out twenty euros and stared into the wallet for so long that his companions thought he was hypnotised by the sight.

"Joe."

"Are you all right, Joe?"

Logic clicked into place. "English money. That's it!"

The women gaped.

"What?"

"What's it?"

"Thanks, young fella." Hurriedly handing twenty euros to Rafael, he urged his companions, "Come on. We have to get back to Apartmentos Ingles quickly."

"Joe. What? Why?"

"Before he scarpers. Because I'm sure he will."

***

Ten minutes later, they hurried into reception to find Ian Dimmock talking earnestly with Christobel.

Her face was serious, but Dimmock was plainly angry. He rounded on Joe and the women. "I hope you're satisfied, Murray."

"I don't have time to chat. Where's—"

"Tom Holgate has gone."

Joe sagged visibly. "Oh, no. We're too late."

"He said he just couldn't take any more after this week, so he packed his bags and left. And it's your fault. All the badgering." The big man bore down on Joe. "He'd been quite content here for years, and all it took was a little snot like you, shoving your nose in where it wasn't wanted to uproot him."

"Oh shut up, you idiot," Brenda ordered. "If you people had had more guts about you, Joe wouldn't have had to shove his nose in, as you put it."

Joe ignored them both, instead, he fumed. "Damn and blast him."

Dimmock appeared satisfied by Joe's irritation. "Did he owe you money or something? I hope so because it's just about what you deserve, Murray."

Joe scowled up at the taller man. "No. He owed nothing, but he owed you an awful lot; all of you. Do me a favour, Dimmock, get your people up to Coyote's. I need to

185

talk to you all. Shall we say fifteen minutes?"

"Why should we? Don't you think we have more to do than …?"

"For me, it's only a matter of pride, but it's a lot more important to you and your friends. A quarter of an hour. Okay?"

Without waiting for a response, Joe and his companions left reception, and made their way up the street to Coyote's.

Fifteen minutes later, with the sun dipping towards the horizon and the cool of evening settling on them, they sat outside the bar, Dimmock and Maurice Keeligan opposite Joe, Sandra with Dimmock, Ann Bamford further along, seated between the Olivants and the Acres. Joe ordered a full round of drinks for the table, and when they were delivered, went into his explanation.

"I owe all you an apology," he said. "Not for any opinion I expressed about your actions or morals. I stand by those. You are all a disgrace to the human race and the British nation, and I'd rather not be associated with you."

"Nice of you to say so," Keeligan grumbled.

"No problem. I said before, I like to tell it as it is." Joe sighed. "But I should apologise for being too slow to realise what was really going on."

A rhubarb murmur ran round the table.

"Each and every one of you was paying Rita Shepperton a substantial sum of money every month. All up she was taking a thousand euros a month from you, and it may be that there are other victims out there we don't know about. The memory stick contains files that we couldn't hack. Now she was no fool, Rita. She knew you could all afford it. Having to pay was an irritation, but it wouldn't bankrupt you, and she could carry on bleeding you for years if she had lived."

"You're stating the obvious, Murray," Dimmock said. "What about it?"

"It wasn't Rita."

186

Another buzz ran round the table, this time accompanied by odd exclamations of surprise and shock.

Joe waited for it to calm down. "I repeat, it wasn't Rita … or at least, it wasn't Rita alone. In fact, it probably wasn't even her idea. It was Holgate."

More exclamations carried through the evening air.

"Is this some kind of excuse for having driven the poor man away?" Sandra Greenwood demanded.

"Do you think I'd care enough about that to drag you all up here?" Joe retorted. "A little while ago, my friend Brenda wanted to leave a tip for the lad who's been looking after us at Chico's all week. Trouble is, we're going home tomorrow and she had no euros on her. Only sterling. That's when it dawned on me. What use is sterling out here? None at all. One of you even said the same to me a few days ago."

Keeligan tutted. "You're still stating the bleeding obvious, man."

Joe ignored him. "You all told me how much you were paying Rita. Two hundred euros a month each. But when I spoke to Holgate, he insisted she was taking five hundred from him, and it was five hundred *pounds*, not euros. But as I've already said, what use is sterling here? Okay, so I know she could have taken English money and gone to the banks or one of the little *cambio* kiosks and shops, but if she'd turned up regularly with large amounts of English money, they would have started to ask questions. I believe Holgate told me she was taking five hundred pounds because he wanted to lay it on really thick, trying to convince me that he was being made to suffer. In truth, he was probably paying her nothing. I can't prove it, because he's gone, but he was probably splitting the take fifty-fifty with Rita every month. Five hundred euros a month would pay his rent here."

A stunned silence greeted the announcement.

"How can you be sure?" Ann Bamford asked.

Joe drank a mouthful of lemonade. "He's done a runner so I

can only speculate, and my ideas stem from the chain of events which brought you all here. Rita came first, and after her, with the exception of Ann, each and every one of you was approached by Holgate. He found you, one by one and invited you to rent an apartment here. Do we assume it was no more than coincidence? Three couples and two individuals, all known to be comparatively well set up. People with something to hide, people wanting to stay away from the glare of publicity." He looked at Maurice. "People too naïve to cover their shady actions. It's a pretty thin coincidence if you ask me. My feeling is he came looking for you. Deliberately seeking you out, and once you were here, the blackmail started." He scanned the table. "You all moved in within a short space of time of each other, and about a year later, she began to blackmail you. And, of course, Holgate would have to claim he was being blackmailed too, to make you believe it was Rita alone." Joe shook his head sadly. "Unless the police catch up with him, which is unlikely, you'll never get to the whole truth, but he's legged it and that's a sure sign of guilt."

"Are you saying he killed Rita?" Keeligan asked.

"I don't know," Joe replied. "I think he did. I asked earlier what happened to Rita's aspirin, and no one answered me. Maurice, did you ever get the prescription filled?"

Keeligan nodded. "The minute she came home from the hospital, and it was filled a second time just a couple of weeks back."

"And yet Terrones couldn't find them, and none of you know what happened to them. Without them, a second heart attack was a near certainty. I think Holgate probably stole them, and eventually, she had the heart attack he'd been expecting, but unless you could get him to admit it, you'd never prove that he was responsible. And when she died, he put the next stage of the operation into action. It was a clever move. He persuaded you all that if you could get at the files she held, the blackmail would end. He roped all of you into this plot to move her body and make it look as if she had been for an early morning swim. What he really wanted was to get at the information for himself."

"But why?" Acre demanded. "I mean if he'd been working with her for so long, as you claim, why did he suddenly decide to kill her?"

"Because she told him she had a daughter. Her name is Felicity and I'm willing to bet that Rita had said if anything happened to her, Felicity would come out here to take over." Joe fidgeted with his drink. "There's this nonsense about honour amongst thieves. It doesn't exist. I don't know anything of the history behind their relationship, but neither of them trusted the other. Holgate did his bit dragging you all here and digging the dirt on you, while Rita applied the pressure. But she kept all the information hidden in her files, and she wouldn't let Holgate have access to them. Instead they were there for her daughter if and when she arrived to take over. I believe Holgate decided he didn't want to be working with the daughter. He wanted it all for himself. He told me his funds were getting low after the financial meltdown of 2008. Dimmock, you're the investment counsellor here. Did you handle Holgate's money?"

"No. He assured me he knew what he was doing, but I know some of the stock he'd invested in has performed pretty poorly this last year or more."

"Down on his uppers," Joe said. "Maybe he felt that if he could get rid of Rita he could have the whole thousand a month for himself."

"But we would have known," Keeligan objected.

"Would you?" Joe asked. "Imagine the situation. Rita is dead. You helped him move her so that her apartment wouldn't be searched too closely by the cops. You all went back the following night looking for the file, but just suppose he had been in earlier in the day and already found it. He had the key, remember. You were probably meant to come away empty-handed that night, but as luck would have it, I beat him to it and I already had the files. Imagine if he had them instead. He didn't need to tell you, did he? So you're all celebrating. Ding dong the witch is dead, but you're still worried that you never found the files. A month later, Holgate approaches you and says Rita's daughter has been in touch and nothing has changed. Except that now it's hard cash, not groceries or prescriptions. You pay him and he'll pass the money on to Felicity. You'd never see her and the money would go straight into Holgate's pockets. If any of you got suspicious later, or demanded to see the daughter, he could disappear in a matter of an hour." He addressed Sandra. "You offered me ten thousand earlier for the memory stick. Whose idea was that?"

Dimmock fumed. "Holgate's." He glowered at Joe. "If you'd agreed, he would have been in a mess."

"Would he? There's a reference in one of Rita's files to the effect that like most men, Holgate talked in bed. That's how I knew he and her had had an affair. Now think about that. Do you imagine that he didn't know the files were stored on a memory stick?"

"Holgate was illiterate when it came to computers," Michael Acre protested.

"I think not," Joe retorted. "It's difficult to pretend to be an expert in any field, but it's easy to pretend to be a complete numpty. I've already said I believe he tracked you down one by one. How did he do that? He used the internet. Remember, I'm speculating, here. He knew about computers, he knew how Rita stored her information. If I'd taken your money and handed over the memory stick, what's the betting he had a spare in his pocket? He picks Rita's up, examines it, says something like, 'so all the information is stored on this little thing', and then he accidentally drops it. He bends to pick it up and with a little sleight of hand he swaps it for a blank stick, which you watch him smash up."

"And how would he have explained this Felicity coming for

more money?" Olivant challenged.

"Simple enough. Felicity is Rita's daughter and she had a copy of everything. He may even have had some woman in the background waiting to come and play the part of Felicity. I don't know. But when I refused the ten grand, he knew his bolt was shot. He still didn't have the files despite all his work. It was time to disappear before he was exposed." Joe glared at Dimmock. "And that is the real reason he left in such a hurry."

"So what now?" Olivant asked. "Now that he's gone, what happens? He still knows so much about us. He could put it all together again and come back."

"What happens is up to you." Joe fished into his shirt pocket and pulled out the memory stick. "All the information Rita had on you is here. There are other files on it which I haven't been able to crack. They may implicate Holgate, they may highlight other victims, I don't know." He passed it to Sandra Greenwood. "I'll leave it with you." Addressing the whole of the table, he went on, "In many ways you've been the architects of your own downfall, all of you. You have skeletons in your cupboards and your determination to escape the publicity surrounding those skeletons gave Holgate and Rita the opportunity to fleece you. The only chance you have of ever bringing Holgate to justice – assuming the Spanish police can find him – is by facing up to your demons. I run a business and I get stick from people all the time. They call me something rotten, but you know something, there's nothing about me you can tell me that I don't already know, and what's more, I don't give a damn who else knows. That means I can never be blackmailed. If you take my advice, you'll hand that over to Terrones and tell him everything."

Chapter Sixteen

October came in heralded by vicious weather, the whole country lashed with high winds and heavy rain.

Ignoring medical advice, Joe was back behind the counter at the Lazy Luncheonette within two days of returning from Torremolinos, but it was a more relaxed Joe, basking in the good natured ribbing of the draymen who commented constantly on his tan, comparing it variously to rust or a coat of creosote.

His tobacco cravings were significantly lower and although he could still be seen taking a crafty drag now and then, no one had actually seen him with a cigarette since the day of his faux heart attack.

But if one thing bothered him, it was the lack of closure on the Apartmentos Ingles affair.

And then, out of the blue, at the turn of the month, he greeted his companions with news.

"I had an email from Sandra Greenwood last night," he said as they prepared to open up for the morning rush.

"Good news?" Sheila asked.

"It depends how you define good," Joe replied. "After we left, they all decided that their secrecy was of lesser importance than bringing Holgate to justice, so they went to Terrones with Rita's files, and Terrones got back to them yesterday. He had tracked down the daughter, living in Germany, and she gave them the password to those files we hadn't been able to get into."

Setting out condiments on the tables, Brenda and Sheila

were suddenly alert.

"And?" Brenda demanded.

"According to Rita, Tim Collins was an invention," Joe told them. "Holgate really did rip the punters off in Derby all those years ago, but he'd managed to fool the police into believing that Collins existed. When Terrones and his people checked Holgate's apartment, they found two bottles of seventy-five milligram aspirin, the low dose stuff Rita was supposed to take to support her heart after the last wobbler. He must have substituted them, with something else. She was bad at taking her pills anyway, but when she did take them, she was probably swallowing chalk or something. Her heart wasn't getting the support it needed and, like I said, it gave out."

"So technically, he murdered her."

Joe nodded. "Terrones also found a range of memory sticks, all of them blank, all of them looking like the one Rita had. I had it right. He knew exactly what he was doing with computers. They've also learned that Rita's late husband was one of the buyers Holgate had taken in, and when she came to the Costa del Sol it was to look for Holgate … or Tim Collins. She found him and threatened to go to the cops with everything she knew. He'd been living there for over twenty years by that time, and he was running out of cash, so he talked her round and suggested they could both make a killing down there by blackmailing others. Rita was all for it, and over the years she stood to make back more than the ten grand her husband had lost in Derby. But she never really trusted Holgate, so she kept all the dirt on him in those files. And she made sure Holgate knew about it. She figured that if he was willing to steal all that money, willing to blackmail others, he might not stop short at murder, and the files were her insurance policy. If she died, her daughter got the goods and only the daughter would know where to look for the file. Even if Holgate found the memory stick, which was unlikely, only Felicity would know how to get into them. Rita didn't apologise for blackmailing the others, so in my book, that makes her almost as bad as Holgate, but you never know what Felicity, the daughter, might have done with the information. She might have handed it to the cops."

"So what's happening?" Sheila asked. "Have they found Holgate?"

Joe shook his head. "Not according to Sandra. But they've put out a European arrest warrant on him. If he puts his head up anywhere in the EU, they'll have him. He's now officially wanted in Spain on charges of extortion and on suspicion of murder, and of course, he's still wanted in England on charges of fraud and deception, and obtaining money under false pretences in the 1980s."

"He'll spend a long time in prison," Brenda said.

"If they ever get him."

Sheila tutted. "You did well, Joe. Remember, he was a very experienced conman. This is closure of a sort, so don't be too disheartened."

"I'm annoyed with myself, Sheila. He was good, I'll grant you, but he managed to con me into believing him, and that galls."

"Yes, well, he's not the only conman is he, Joe?" Brenda said.

"What's that supposed to mean?"

"I'm talking about you and your non-smoking. You are smoking, aren't you?"

"Yes, but—"

"Don't lie, Joe. We know. We saw you smoking several times in Torremolinos, and we've spotted you taking a sly smoke here."

Joe fished into his pockets and held up the cigarette. "You mean this?"

Both women scowled their disapproval.

With a grin, Joe tossed it across the room. "Here. Catch."

Taken by surprise Brenda only just managed to catch it. To her surprise, she found it long, sturdier than a normal cigarette, fabricated from strong plastic.

"Oh," she said. "It's an electronic cigarette."

"It gives me some of the kick without most of the chemicals. And it gives me something to do with my hands," Joe told her. "That way I keep them off you."

Brenda smiled coyly. "Ooh, Joe, fancy you wanting to put your hands on me."

Sheila laughed.

Joe, too, smiled. "I meant round your throat."

THE END

Fantastic Books
Great Authors

Meet our authors and discover our exciting range:

- Gripping Thrillers
- Cosy Mysteries
- Romantic Chick-Lit
- Fascinating Historicals
- Exciting Fantasy
- Young Adult and Children's Adventures

Visit us at:
www.crookedcatpublishing.com

Join us on facebook:
www.facebook.com/crookedcatpublishing

15801685R00119

Printed in Great Britain
by Amazon